Tiny

Easy lad

Chapter One

'All rise.'

As the gavel dropped, Horatio Tiny stood, slowly bowed his head in respect to the Queen and the barristers before him, and turned towards the little wooden door to the right of the bench. As he left the court for the last time, he made his way back to his chambers soaking in the character of the stone walls and ancient leaded glass windows. He had been serving as a high court judge for the past eleven years and was puzzled why he hadn't taken more notice of his surroundings. Of course, he hadn't intended to become a judge; well, he dreamed perhaps one day, but during the bleak and tiring days of the war, he would have been quite happy with a quiet job as a humble country solicitor. It was 1985 and the world was changing. Greed was apparently good and life was turning cruel. It certainly wasn't the world Tiny had expected to see.

Back in his private chambers, Tiny paused at the large mirror in the hall. As he stared at himself, he could see his father looking back. Where had the years gone? His hair had turned white around the edges. The lines which had once sat lightly upon his face were now drawn deep and distinct. He tried hard to look after himself with a healthy lifestyle and exercise, but though he still maintained his slim physique, it was clear age was gaining the upper hand. He felt age had accelerated since his beloved Patricia had passed, but in reality, he was probably just more aware of it since being on his own.

Having changed back into ordinary clothes, he met his brother judges for a celebratory retirement drink in the chambers of the Recorder of London. Tiny hated fuss, and would rather have slipped out the rear door without anyone noticing but he felt he should be sociable. 'Everyone loves a party,' he could hear the others say. Well actually no; Tiny could think of little worse.

"Come in, come in my dear fellow." The Recorder of London was obviously pleased to see him. "And a good result for your last case," he added.

Not if you were the accused, Tiny thought sarcastically. "Yes indeed," he exclaimed with a smile, secretly wondering how short a time he could stay without appearing rude.

Apart from the Recorder of London (the most senior judge), the Common Serjeant of London (his number two), and four other judges (all smiling), there were a couple of senior barristers, (neither of whom he particularly got along with), and a sprinkling of clerks. They are only here to make sure I'm actually leaving, Tiny cynically surmised as he sipped his Campari and soda; that and of course the free buffet. A few bridge rolls, some vol-au-vents of dubious quality and some cheese and pineapple on sticks hardly qualified as a buffet, but there it was in all its glory. It was obviously the State hadn't pushed the boat out, but nevertheless it was a kind thought and Tiny took the gesture as it was intended.

"So, what are you going to do with yourself?" asked one of the more helpful clerks.

"I'm moving to the country," Tiny declared with a certainty that disguised months of indecision.

Although firmly established in London for many years, Tiny always considered himself to be a country lad at heart. Born in Cirencester, Gloucestershire in the summer of 1919, he spent most his childhood either rummaging amongst the hedgerows or speeding along the country lane on his ever-so-modern bicycle. Helping out with the horses on a local farm during school holidays, Tiny had once considered a life on the land however being one of the many babies born following the Great War, there was so much hope for the future. The world was evolving at a rapid pace and the 1914 – 1918 conflict was the catalyst. The good times predicted didn't quite turn out as planned, although the traditional approach to hierarchy had diminished considerably. After the heady days of the 1960s, 70s and now the 80s, the mere thought of the year 1919 seemed a millennium away, like an historical event you would read about in a novel, or perhaps a caption on an old black and white photograph, where everyone looks so stern, dressed in their Sunday best. How times had changed. Saying that, for Cirencester a mere sixty-six years was a blink of the eye, a measly pin-prick in the depths of time.

Dating back to the days before the Romans, Cirencester had always been a delightfully cultured town. 'Capital of the Cotswolds,' it proudly claimed, despite nearly slipping off the area's most south-westerly edge. Saying that, Tiny loved the area, and after being away at boarding school for several

3

years, he was glad to return home to spend many a happy hour wandering through the Abbey grounds contemplating what to do with his life. Still unsure, and under pressure from his parents, Tiny enrolled (or more accurately 'was enrolled') at Merton College, Oxford to read Jurisprudence. One of the great benefits of Oxford was its relative proximity to Cirencester which allowed Tiny the opportunity to visit home whenever he chose. It also shared many of the same features as Cirencester albeit on a much grander scale, and its familiar feel, made Tiny feel at home. It was 1937, and rumours of war were already starting to gain momentum.

Tiny was a reluctant conscript but after most of his year group signed up and the remainder were about to receive their call-up papers, Tiny felt he had little choice other than to volunteer. He spent many a sleepless night trying to decide how to do his bit without being killed. It wasn't that he didn't support the war, and of course the Nazi regime needed to be stopped, but Tiny had no desire to be a hero and was quite happy for others to take the lead role.

No matter how hard he tried, Tiny always felt a little different from his peers. A deep thinker, he was friendly and wanted to join in, although he always felt a little awkward in social situations. In fact, the larger the event, the more awkward he felt. There were times however, when he needed to be part of the group, and this was one such occasion. He decided to opt for the RAF as the least worst option, and after putting his studies on hold, was duly dispatched to Cranwell.

If the truth is told, he found the whole experience fairly mundane. Learning to fly was quite straightforward, although he did suffer his fair share of bumpy landings. Little attention was paid to the technical aspect of flying, which was unfortunate especially as he found this aspect far more interesting. When the rest of his group were eventually dispersed to join various squadrons, Tiny was taken to one side and introduced to the relatively new activity of photographic reconnaissance. Stationed at RAF Medmenham in Buckinghamshire, Tiny enjoyed the splendours of Danesfield House where he spent five interesting but equally tedious years flying first Mosquitoes and later Mark XI Spitfires. Neither were fitted with guns or armaments of any description, which at the time suited Tiny just fine. It was only upon reflection that he considered this to be a little unfair, especially as the Germans seem to have plenty of firepower which they used in abundance. He found it quite ironic that despite flying Spitfires for a large part of the war, he never actually had the opportunity to shoot at anyone, although secretly he was quite thankful. The only positive that came from the whole episode was meeting Patricia, a lovely auburn beauty with a grace and elegance Tiny had never previously encountered. Exquisite in every way, Patricia worked as a photographic interpreter and over the five years of the war, they became inseparable.

The RAF is a strange institution, although quite young as a service when Tiny joined; he puzzled as to why they were so keen to portray an air of tradition. One such custom involved the allocation of valets, or as they were more commonly known, batmen. It was while he was at Danefield House that Tiny first met George Rawlings, a corporal with the Wiltshire Regiment, injured while escaping Dunkirk. Rawlings's role was to look after the officers stationed at RAF Medmenham and although Tiny shared him with three other officers, he seemed to generate an added level of respect from Rawlings which lasted throughout their time together. Later, when Tiny was promoted to squadron leader, Rawlings was assigned to look after him alone, leading to an even closer rapport.

As the war ended, the comrades went their separate ways. Tiny and Patricia married, and remained so until Patricia's untimely death in 1983 from a brain tumour; she was 63.

Rawlings also married, and divorced (twice), but never really settled, and bounced from job to job. Conversely, Tiny established himself in the legal profession, and after completing his studies, joined Trinity Chambers based at Inner Temple. Appointed QC in 1966 aged 47, he was called to the bench in 1974, and it was Christmas that year during a seasonal event at the Grosvenor House Hotel on Park Lane that the two comrades were reunited.

"Mr Rawlings?" Tiny enquired with a disbelieving look of astonishment.

Tiny had always treated Rawlings with respect and used his correct title. Even during their time together at RAF Medmenham when it should have been Corporal, Tiny insisted on addressing Rawlings as Mr. Although it had been nearly thirty years, there was no mistaking his old comrade.

"Well I never! Good evening, sir. This is surprise," Rawlings replied with a broad smile.

Rawlings worked as part of the concierge team and had been at the hotel for the past two years. As the crowds surged past, they didn't have time to chat although they caught up later and reminisced about old times.

As a new judge, and having an increasing number of social engagements to attend, Tiny was entitled to a driver. He no longer had the time to manage to the day-to-day minutiae and had been considering seeking help for some while. This chance encounter seemed almost fate in its timing, and after agreeing terms with the Ministry, and of course gaining approval from Patricia, Rawlings left his employment at the Grosvenor House Hotel and was assigned to look after Tiny and collected him each morning from his house, just around the corner at 37 Park Street, Mayfair.

Rawlings didn't really consider the job to be work. It was the only time since he was demobbed that he actually felt happy. He remained with Tiny through the years, helping him as his career progressed and supporting him through the dark days following Patricia's death. Working for Tiny wasn't always easy, but Rawlings felt at home; he had finally found his place in the world. He felt comfortable, settled and content; it was as if it was meant to be.

Tiny appreciated Rawlings support more than words could say, but rarely acknowledged it. Although it was now more than two years since Tiny lost his beloved Patricia, the memory was as fresh as ever. Nursing her through her illness, and watching her decline, had taken its toll. As Patricia's brain tumour developed it first robbed her of her mobility, then her speech, and finally her consciousness.

Dying with dignity is a misnomer Tiny thought bitterly; there is no such thing. As he struggled to recover, the house he once loved became a cold and uncomfortable mass of bricks and irrelevant objects. Tiny started to hate the place; everywhere he looked it reminded him of Patricia. It was empty; the laughter and life had gone. Tiny almost unconsciously found himself talking to Patricia as if she was still there. Of course, he knew she wasn't, but in a way, it was comforting. Bedtime was the worst. Turning off the lights made the house seem even larger, emptier, and in a strange way a little intimidating. Although sometimes a comfort, the memories made it too painful to remain. Tiny tried to be philosophical but the loneliness and isolation fuelled his decision to stand down from the bench and move out of London. He didn't know what the future held, but he knew it was time to move on.

The party was gaining momentum, and as the volume of conversation increased to near deafening levels, Tiny's thoughts began to drift.

"Shall I bring the car around, sir?" enquired Rawlings.

Suddenly Tiny was snapped back into the present. "That would be timely, Mr Rawlings. Thank you."

Rawlings didn't need to be told when Tiny was ready to go. Their relationship built up over the years negated the need for words although politeness ensured they remained.

As Tiny made his apologies, respectfully resisting his colleagues' insistence that he stay, he gathered his coat, and bidding farewell to his old life, left the Central Criminal Court for the last time by a discreet rear entrance.

Chapter Two

A gentle infusion of classical music awoke Tiny at his usual hour. Although it wasn't a work day (he had left that behind several weeks ago), it was still going to be a busy one. After nineteen years at 37 Park Street this was his last morning. The removal team were booked and due at 10.00 am. Although he was pretty much packed and ready to go, there were still a few last items that Tiny couldn't bring himself to remove from their rightful position. A home is more than a collection of items, he thought to himself and everywhere he looked he could see memories. He smiled as thoughts of Patricia filled his mind. If the truth be told, thoughts of Patricia were never far away; a comfort in one way, a hurtful memory in another.

It really didn't seem like two years since Patricia's passing; everywhere Tiny looked he could see his beloved wife. He felt a considerable twinge of guilt over selling the house, although he knew Patricia would have scolded him for being so sentimental. Even knowing what she would have thought, he couldn't help feeling he was selling her as well, throwing her out of his life forever and turning his back on all the good times they had spent together.

As he prepared himself for the day, he sat over his bowl of porridge waiting for his usual pot of English breakfast tea to brew. He had stopped the papers at the beginning of the week and felt a little lost without anything to read.

After finishing his breakfast, Tiny gathered the last few items together and waited patiently for Maurice Inch and his brothers to arrive. Inch & Bros (Removals) Ltd had been recommended by Rawlings as a reliable and reasonable team of 'lifters & shifters'. Tiny was amused by this description and, not knowing anyone else, decided they would be as good as anyone.

Tiny paced across his hall impatiently looking at his watch. He smiled to himself; he knew time wasn't going to move any faster if he kept looking, but he really couldn't stop himself. As he waited nervously, he wanted to check his appearance, but annoyingly the hallway mirror was already packed. Tiny prided himself on his appearance even when there was really no need to look smart, and was slightly irritated that there was nothing in the house to reassure him.

A loud bang on the brass knocker returned him to his senses. As Tiny opened the door he was greeted by a thinly built, greying man standing in the entrance. Dressed in a brown tradesman's coat with a coke proudly perched on his head, the man smiled as he slowly lifted his hat.

"Good morning, sir. Maurice Inch at your service."

This was it; it has started. The end of a life in London suddenly seemed real.

Tiny had spent weeks methodically assembling his entire life into a neat collection of boxes. Whilst everything in the house was in order, there was also his car to consider.

Although he didn't drive much in London (he had Rawlings for that), he knew he would need a car in the country. In a rather impetuous moment, he had decided to purchase a brand-new vehicle for his future life. He had chosen a traditional British Morgan Plus Four, although when he placed his order, he hadn't realised there was a waiting list. Despite having ordered it well over a year ago, the car had only just arrived, and apart from a quick spin around Mayfair, Tiny hadn't ventured any further in it. It looked a treat, he thought to himself; indigo blue with cream leather interior. Tiny thought it was the cats' whiskers. He knew Patricia would have smiled disapprovingly if she had known what he had bought, but he thought why not. Frivolous and impractical maybe; but it was fun, and rather snazzy. It had been parked in the street since it had arrived, which made Tiny rather nervous. He was grateful his new house had a garage. All the same, the prospect of driving all the way to Wiltshire was slightly daunting.

As the removal lorry drew away from Park Street, an arm gently waved from the passenger window.

"See you in Wiltshire, your honour," Maurice shouted, his voice fading as the neighbouring traffic filled the void where the lorry had once stood.

Tiny instinctively waved back, although the lorry had already turned into Mount Street and was heading towards Park Lane.

"Good morning, sir," cried a voice from behind him.

Tiny turned. "Mr Rawlings," he replied. "This is an unexpected pleasure."

"Indeed, sir. I have a little time on my hands, and wondered, well... would like me to drive you to Wiltshire?"

Tiny was a little taken back by this offer. It was far too generous, although he had to admit he felt relieved.

"That's very kind, Mr Rawlings, and much appreciated, but surely it's a little out of your way?"

"Not really, sir. I'm heading that way and would be happy to... well, you know... one last time?"

Tiny smiled. "Of course, Mr Rawlings. Thank you, I would be delighted."

Although he was a year younger than Tiny, being of pensionable age, Rawlings didn't really have to option to continue and if he was honest, he didn't really want to. Although the Ministry of Justice thanked him for his service, it was clear that without Tiny to support him, there was no future. His colourful life had taken its toll and he felt all of his sixty-five years, especially as he was a heavy smoker. He had been offered a cottage back on the Ashbury Estate where he was born, and was eager to accept. His parents had worked for the Estate all of their lives, but there was no longer the need for domestic staff. His father had long passed, and as a consequence of his mother moving into a care home, the cottage where Rawlings was raised was now available for rent. In exchange for a little discount, he had agreed to do a few odd jobs for the new owners, plus a little driving work when required.

The Ashbury Estate occupied an enviable setting on the edge of the Marlborough Downs just to the north of Yatesbury. Quite by chance, Tiny's new home in Oakshaw was only about five miles away, and unknown to Tiny, Rawlings had arranged to meet a friend at the Oakshaw Arms for lunch.

As they sped out of London Tiny became even more grateful for Rawlings's offer to drive. As the miles slipped away, the traffic on the M4 thinned. Approaching junction 14, they exited the motorway and took the old A4 through Marlborough and on past Silbury Hill. Just the other side of Avebury, they turned right towards the village of Oakshaw. Although it was still only early March, Tiny insisted Rawlings stop for a moment to lower the hood. He wanted to smell the air of his new life and to immerse himself in the beauty of Wiltshire. Rawlings was less impressed and if the truth was told, wasn't particularly taken with the Morgan. He also considered fresh air to be very overrated. Though the sun shone bright in the clear spring sky, the temperature belied any impression of warmth. It did, however, highlight the beauty of the numerous daffodils strewn along the verges, which for Tiny was reward enough.

Tiny thought Oakshaw was delightful, not chocolate box pretty, but quiet and full of character. He was familiar with the area having spent many a happy holiday walking along the Wansdyke. Although only a short section now survived, the combes along the Marlborough Downs were stunning and were the perfect antidote to a stressful life in London. Oakshaw had only around two hundred residents and was fairly compact, mainly consisting of a collection of brick and flint cottages gathered around a small green which housed the memorial from the Great War. Most of the residents were engaged in traditional farm work or other rural trades, but as the twentieth century marched on, local work had dried up. More and more properties were now being occupied by outsiders seeking a quieter life. Tiny found this quite depressing, before realising he was doing exactly the same.

Getting out of the car, he breathed in the crisp Wiltshire air and gazed around the village. The fourteenth century church stood proudly to the west on a slight incline. The Oakshaw Garage, a rather scruffy and dated business, occupied an imposing position towards the north and was adjacent to the main road from Chippenham to Swindon. Thankfully, over the years the road had been rerouted to the far side of the village, so what was once the front of the garage was now the rear. The Oakshaw Arms had benefited in a similar way, with a quiet rear garden disguising the busy entrance and car park beyond. As traffic volume, and speed, increased over the years, Tiny was thankful that the discrete heart of the village remained obscured and blissfully quiet.

Tiny had fallen in love with Bourne House during his first viewing. As the estate agent remarked at the time, people usually make up their mind about a new property within the first three minutes of walking through the door; Tiny broke the record; he had made his decision before he reached the front door. It was the only Georgian style house in the village, but the weathered brick blended perfectly with the surrounding cottages. Tiny appreciated symmetry, and the even balance of windows on either side of the imposing front door indicated the classic layout of the house behind. Over the years, most of the properties within the village had suffered various extensions and not always sympathetically. Bourne House had not escaped the dreaded home improvement craze, but conversely, it had actually benefited from the imposing orangery added onto the rear. It not only added a welcome source of light, but also offered a third reception room, making the house far more spacious. The kitchen was a particular favourite enjoying an equal blend of traditional and modern features. Saying that, the oil-fired Aga wasn't quite to Tiny's taste in addition to being a tad excessive for a single occupant. The four bedrooms at the top of the central staircase, two on the right; two on the left, were ample to a point of decadence, but he valued space and just loved the character of the house.

The outside was equally appealing. The front garden featured two almost perfect rectangles either side of the front path; the rear was far more interesting. A long sweeping garden narrowed as it met the gentle running stream that separated it from the pastures beyond. Tiny appreciated the privacy of the garden which wasn't overlooked, unless of course you counted the bullocks grazing up to the stream. Despite being a novice, Tiny had always enjoyed gardening and was looking forward to spending peaceful afternoons pottering outside. Most of the garden was laid to grass, with several semi-circular borders of herbaceous perennials on either side of the lawn. An armillary globe stood upon a small area of paving raising both the profile and presence of the garden. A vegetable area to one side was separated by a low-level beech hedge with a small, rather dilapidated greenhouse at one end. Tiny was inexplicably excited at the prospect of a greenhouse, although he didn't really know how or when he was going to use it.

To the side of the house, a double-gated entrance extended to an area that appeared to be originally designed as stabling. Two renovated buildings formed a right angle around a courtyard to the side of the rear garden. One of the buildings had an open front and judging by the oil on the concrete, had recently been used as garaging. The other was more of a mystery, its closed doors disguising any contents laying within. The traditional oak weatherboarding which had once featured on both buildings had sadly been replaced with creosoted softwood, although the original tiled roof remained.

In general, Bourne House was a bit of a misnomer; modern but traditional, spacious yet compact, and quiet whilst in the middle of a bustling village.

"Shall I park the car in the garage for you, sir?" enquired Rawlings.

"That's kind, Mr Rawlings, but maybe just leave it in the drive for now. I'll put it away later. Besides, I'm sure you need to be on your way."

Rawlings bid Tiny farewell and headed off towards the Oakshaw Arms to meet his friend. As Maurice Inch and his team hadn't yet arrived, Tiny decided to open up the house to ensure it was ready to greet his belongings. Although spring was well established, the rooms still felt cold and a little damp. It had been left empty for several months, ever since the previous elderly resident passed away. Tiny fully appreciated the delay caused by probate and the legal process involved in selling a property, but nevertheless houses didn't like being empty; like him, they grew lonely.

Opening the windows downstairs, the spring air rushed in, eagerly filling the house. Tiny then climbed the stairs and repeated the process in the bedrooms. He paused in the main bedroom and peered across the village, his thoughts lingering on the loss of Patricia, and how she would have loved this house.

The whole of humanity was laid out before him. He could see the rear of the Oakshaw Arms, and the beer garden, where a number of guests were willing summer to arrive. The garage too looked busy, as did the village shop on the opposite side of the green. There even appeared to be activity at the church although Tiny quickly realised that this was deceptive as the cars were probably merely overspill from the shop and pub. A wave of contentment drifted across him as he surveyed village life.

His tranquil mood was broken as the familiar blue and yellow removal van pulled up outside. Spotting Tiny at the upstairs window, Maurice Inch raised his arm in greeting. Now the work starts, Tiny thought.

It was around 6.00 pm before Maurice and team had emptied their van and finally headed for home. Tiny was pleased to be on his own, although everywhere he looked there were boxes. Admittedly they were all in the correct rooms, but Tiny felt daunted by the task ahead. He could swear he had fewer boxes when he left London; maybe Maurice had a few left over from a previous client, he thought with a smile.

It had been a long and eventful day and Tiny was tired. He couldn't have mustered the energy to prepare supper even if he'd had food in the house. He hadn't yet unpacked his kitchen items either, so thinking it was a good opportunity to meet some of the locals, he donned his best tweed coat and fedora and headed across the green to the Oakshaw Arms. Silence fell across the room as Tiny entered through the rear door. Walking past an array of mismatching tables, presumably used for dining, he made his way towards the bar. It was an odd sort of place, a quirky blend of ancient and modern. A pool table was situated near to the front door adjacent to the dart board. A real fire was burning in the small Victorian hearth, but the ambience wasn't really improved by the fruit machine located to the side of the bar. He instantly felt at a disadvantage; it was apparent most of the regulars knew exactly who he was, whereas he knew no one. They purposely paused what they were doing as if to stake their territory and establish the upper hand. Undeterred, Tiny continued to the bar.

Conscious of his surroundings, Tiny decided his normal tipple of Campari and soda wasn't appropriate, and wishing to fit in, he thought beer might be more suitable.

"Good evening. A bottle of Guinness if I may, and from the warm shelf if possible?" A smile spread over the face of the man behind the bar.

"You must be His Honour Justice Tiny," the man responded rather smugly. "I saw the removal van earlier."

"Well, yes, but Tiny is just fine," he replied, feeling slightly embarrassed. "Lovely place you have here." Tiny added trying hard not to reveal his true feelings.

The man stretched out a hand. "I'm Tony. The landlord." he announced proudly.

As the evening progressed, Tiny was gradually introduced to most of the locals. It became apparent that there was a regular clique of villagers whose main pastime appeared to centre upon the pub. Tiny was careful to listen, patiently taking an interest in each of their lives. He remembered the words of his old mentor: 'People always find whatever they are saying to you at least ten time more interesting than whatever you say to them.'

After a second bottle of Guinness, and a rather tasty steak and ale pie, Tiny was ready for home. The day was catching up on him and together with the prospect of more unpacking, he felt distinctly weary. As he rose to leave, Mike Warren the local garage owner commented, "Steady as you go, Tiny, you look whacked."

"It's been a long day and there's still a lot to do." Tiny sighed; he had never been good at hiding his tiredness.

"Well, if you are looking for help, my sister does a little cleaning," Mike added.

Tiny smiled. "That would be very much appreciated."

"I'll ask her to call round tomorrow, shall I?"

"Perfect. Thank you Mike," Tiny responded with relief.

As Tiny walked back to his new home, the cold evening air made him pull his scarf a little higher around his neck. He so wished Patricia was there to help him along the way, but alas, he was alone and facing a new life without her. The tranquillity of Oakshaw was oddly reassuring and unnerving in equal measure, although after meeting some of his new neighbours he was already beginning to feel part of the community. He smiled to himself as the light from the pub was slowly replaced by the inky black of the night sky. The gentle scrunch of the dew-soaked grass under his feet and the lack of streetlamps seemed strangely unfamiliar however, the feeling of equanimity and inner peace kept the worst of the evening chill at bay.

Chapter Three

As Tiny pulled back the curtains, another bright and crisp morning greeted him. A slight frost made the grass white in all but the brightest spots, although the sun was already at work painting nature's canvas with greens, yellows and blues. The daffodils stood triumphantly across the village and stretched right up to the door of the church on the opposite side of the green. The combination of dew and the thawing frost made everything glisten.

There was already activity at the garage as residents left their cars on the forecourt ready for Mike and his team to perform their mechanical magic. The pub unsurprisingly appeared quiet, but the Oakshaw Village Shop and Post Office was open, and the proprietor Mr Trevor Stubbs was busy sorting the newspapers for the day's deliveries. Embracing the fresh air of the day, Tiny decided to head across to the village shop for a morning paper. He so enjoyed thumbing through the inky pages of The Times over a coffee and catching up on all the latest scandal. Being an early bird, Trevor didn't often frequent the Oakshaw Arms, preferring to spend time with his family. All the same, Trevor seemed to be a sociable chap. Constantly cheerful, he always saw the good in people and enjoyed nothing more than a chat with his customers. Tiny wondered how this was possible; he himself had seen so much crime and hurt that he tended to view life with suspicion and mistrust. He secretly envied Trevor and smiled at the idyllic and tranquil sight that was laid out before him. All was well with the world.

It was around 10.30 am when Tiny heard a knock at the door. Without much thought, he ceased his unpacking and moved through the hall to greet his caller. A sense of puzzlement came over him as he approached the door as he wasn't expecting visitors, especially as he didn't actually know anyone yet. Upon opening the door, a short, rather rotund lady dressed in a blue/grey tweed overcoat, stood before him.

"Good morning, Mr Tiny. Sorry to bother you; my brother, Mike asked me to stop by... You need a little help with your cleaning I believe?" The lady enquired with a degree of nervousness that Tiny found quite endearing.

"Oh yes, thank you," he responded. "Please, just call me Tiny; you are?"

"I'm Margaret," the lady replied. "Shall I come in?"

Tiny smiled at the self-invitation but was grateful for the offer of assistance.

Margaret was a most interesting character. Her husband Robert drove the local taxi, and he and Mike were best friends and well known throughout the village. Tiny quickly learned that Margaret had been born in Oakshaw and had rarely ventured beyond its confines. A true local, she seemed to know something about everyone and recited endless stories most of which seemed to be based upon gossip combined with copious amounts of conjecture conveniently added to fill any gaps. Tiny surprised himself by enjoying her company, and quickly began to rely upon Margaret's weekly visits.

It was a wet Thursday morning in late April when the familiar rattle of keys opened the front door and Margaret hurried in as usual. Today, however, Tiny instantly knew something was wrong.

"Are you OK, Margaret?" he enquired, a little worried.

"Oh Mr Tiny!" Margaret exclaimed, bursting into tears. It was only the second time Margaret had referred to Tiny as 'Mr' so he knew something was different.

Tiny decided it was his turn to make the tea. Sitting Margaret at the kitchen table in front of the Aga, he tried to comfort her.

Although incoherent at first, Tiny slowly began to comprehend the problem. Gradually putting the pieces together, he started to understand why Margaret was so upset. Her nephew Stephen Cole, a stable lad, had been killed while working at the local racing stables. When Tiny heard the name Ashbury Estate his interest spiked, and he wondered whether his old comrade Mr Rawlings was aware. It later transpired that the whole village seemed to know, although when Tiny applied a little logic, and considered the nature of the area and how quickly news travelled, it really shouldn't have been a surprise.

As Margaret explained a little more, Tiny's interest morphed into intrigue. "I just don't understand it, Mr Tiny," Margaret continued (third time she had used 'Mr'). "His horses were like family to him, and for it to happen in the stables, well, it just doesn't seem right." She broke down and sobbed.

"I'm sure the police will investigate," Tiny said reassuringly. "Sometimes these things just happen. Horses can be very unpredictable," he added, trying to sound like he knew something about racehorses, which of course he didn't.

Margaret turned her head towards Tiny, and stared at him directly through tearful eyes, "Oh Mr Tiny," she sobbed, (fourth) "will you speak with the police for me and ask them what happened? They are saying it's an accident but I just can't believe it. My sister and her husband live in Australia and there's no one here to help. Robert doesn't know what to do and I have no one else to ask. Please...." Margaret pleaded finally beginning to sound like her old self.

"I'm not sure if there's anything I can do," Tiny muttered sympathetically. "I have no influence over the police, and besides, I'm sure they have matters in hand." He added, "If they are saying it's an accident, there's nothing any of us can do." He added with a sense of authority.

"Well, it just doesn't seem right." Margaret paused. "I think there's more to it. There's been lots of stories about those new owners." Margaret added with a frown. "I'm sorry, Tiny, I think I should go home now, I'm too upset to work today," she added, rising from her chair. As she entered the cold dampness of a thoroughly miserable day, Margaret turned to Tiny and said with determination, "It just doesn't seem right." and then with a quiet sense of vulnerability, repeated in a whisper, "It just doesn't seem right," With that, Margaret disappeared into the gloom leaving Tiny holding the door in stunned silence.

As the day slipped by, Tiny busied himself with this and that, but no matter how he tried, his thoughts kept returning to their conversation. He had become quite fond of Margaret over the past few weeks and felt dreadfully sad for her and her family. With the parents so far away, of course Margaret felt responsible. Understandable really, he thought as he tried to reassure himself that the police had the situation in hand. Besides, what could he do? Applying a little rational thought, he dismissed the matter from his mind, determined not to get involved. Although he was well versed with the aftermath of tragedy, he had hoped all that was behind him. Experiencing it in Oakshaw wasn't what Tiny had expected and if the truth was known, it unsettled him a little.

A couple of days later, Tiny paid one of his regular, well semi-regular, early evening visits to the Oakshaw Arms. He usually called in about once a week, just to be sociable and more importantly, not to appear aloof to the villagers. Rather surprisingly, he quite enjoyed his visits and liked the fact that the landlord Tony reached for a bottle of Guinness (off the warm shelf, naturally) as soon as Tiny walked through the door. He almost felt like a local, but in his heart, he knew he would have to be at least second generation to be fully accepted.

The pub was busier than normal; Mike, Robert and even Trevor all sat around the fire with several empty beer glasses nearby. As expected, talk of the unfortunate demise of

Stephen Cole was the main, nay, the only topic of conversation. Tiny tried not to get involved but listened intently. Straining to hear, he couldn't quite make out everything that was being said, but it was obviously that there was no love lost for the new owners of the Ashbury Estate. Having changed hands around eighteen months previous, the estate was now owned by an American couple who had developed the equestrian side of the business at the expense of the more usual arable and mixed livestock. Now a stud and racing stables, thoroughbreds from the Ashbury Estate were apparently making quite a name for themselves both domestically and internationally. Rather than traditional estate activities the new owners had converted most of the arable land into pasture and gallops for their racing stock. Gone was the long-established shoot, along with most of the heavy farm equipment. Apparently, most of the barns that once housed the farm implements were now full of feed and straw for bedding.

Tiny was learning quite a lot although he cynically only half believed what he was hearing. It was, however, quite apparent that there had been considerable investment to develop this new venture. According to local gossip (which of course Tiny never listened to), the new owners were equally known for the treatment of their staff, although not in a good way. It seemed that everyone knew someone who was either working or had worked for the Ashbury Estate.

Tiny slowly sipped his Guinness, not commenting on or participating in the ongoing saga. He was, what could be described, as mildly intrigued, but had no intention of interfering. With no knowledge of the equestrian world, and never having visited the Ashbury Estate, Tiny didn't want to ruffle any feathers. He was trying to live a quiet life and settle into the village. Interference from him would not please anyone. He had left the law in London, and if truth was told, he was rather tired of policemen and their antics. He still felt sorry for Margaret, and as he tussled with his thoughts, he found his earlier determination not to get involved beginning to waver. I suppose a little look around wouldn't hurt and I haven't seen Rawlings for a while, he thought. Besides, the Morgan would probably benefit from a little exercise.

With a decisive final sip of his Guinness, his mind was set. He wished a good evening to his comrades, and without giving any clue to his intentions, he quietly left the Oakshaw Arms and headed for home.

Chapter Four

Tiny woke to a bright spring morning, although a little overnight rain lingered in puddles along the sides of the road. It was fast approaching the end of April. Easter was a fading memory, and although winter held on to early mornings and the ever-shortening nights, it was clear it would soon lose out to the summer ahead.

As Tiny surveyed the scene before him, a broad smile crept over his face. Oh, good, he thought, I can put the roof down. Tiny loved his Morgan and although he didn't really drive it as much as he would have liked, he dropped the roof at every opportunity. After a light breakfast he telephoned Rawlings, and they arranged to meet on the Ashbury Estate at 10.30 that morning.

Rawlings didn't really give the matter much thought. He was pleased to hear from his old mentor and never suspected any ulterior motive. The Ashbury Estate was only five miles from Oakshaw and should have taken Tiny around fifteen minutes, but when Rawlings glanced at his watch, it was already 10.33 and Tiny was nowhere to be seen.

The journey may have been short but it consisted of twisting country roads and leafy lanes, and whilst a delight to drive, (Tiny would have been happy to have extended the experience) he prided himself on punctuality.

Diligently following the signs, he turned at the entrance to Ashbury Hall, the main house on the estate. After winding his way along the long gravel drive for around one quarter of a mile, he eventually arrived at the large imposing stone house that probably dated from the mid to late eighteenth century. Rather strangely, the main entrance appeared to be at the rear of the house along with a sizeable gravel area for parking.

Tiny pulled the cast iron door bell, and faintly heard it ring on the inside. He became increasingly irritated as the minutes slipped by and still no one came to the door. He was just about to repeat the process as the well-worn, heavy oak door creaked open. An elderly man appeared who, upon seeing Tiny's hand on the doorbell, raised his eyebrows disapprovingly. "Yes?" he enquired pompously.

It quickly became apparent that he was one of the many domestic assistants and that for 'staff enquiries' Tiny should have taken the tradesmen's entrance. Although there was undoubtedly access within the grounds, he was directed back to the main road along with strict instructions.

"Turn right at the end of the drive, proceed four hundred yards along the road, then turn right by the village hall, and after half a mile right again." The command was delivered with no room for debate.

Tiny smiled, thanked the elderly gentleman politely and returned to his Morgan. As he retraced his journey back along the drive, he tried hard to suppress a slight annoyance made worse by the knowledge that he was now uncharacteristically very late.

Following the directions as instructed, his irritation grew as he saw a bold sign announcing 'Tradesmen's Entrance' which considering the narrow, muddy and remote nature of the lane, was the only turning to anywhere. Tiny prided himself in his impartiality, his career had depended upon it, however he already had a poor opinion of the Ashbury Estate especially as his pristine Morgan was spattered in mud.

Upon reaching the appropriate entrance, he slowly weaved his way down the drive. The ambience couldn't have been more different from the lane outside. Immaculately manicured grass bordered freshly painted post and rail fencing, and beyond lay paddocks and lush, velvety meadows. As Tiny approached the stable yard he noticed an identical pair of semi-detached cottages on the right-hand side. All four properties proudly featured doors and windows painted grass green. Well maintained though they were, they didn't really appeal to Tiny's more neutral taste. The gardens at the front of the cottages were divided by a copper beech hedge which prominently stretched along the front. It was apparent that all four cottages had recently benefited from a little modernisation, and the same was true of the far more impressive stable block beyond.

Tiny noticed a gravel pull-in just before the first cottage and brought his Morgan to a halt. As the front wheel sank into a pot-hole with a bump, and yet more mud splashed onto the paintwork, Tiny's irritation intensified.

Rawlings was outside the stables when Tiny arrived. Seeing him parked by his cottage, he started to make his way the short distance back up the drive, carefully avoiding a Ford 4600 tractor that was returning into the yard. Rawlings paused and watched with amusement as his old boss turned off the engine and climbed out of his car, trying clumsily to avoid the mud and puddles. After awkwardly exchanging greetings, Rawlings proudly invited Tiny into his home.

It was an unimposing semi-detached brick cottage, one of many built after the Great War, not huge, but adequate for a couple and generous for one. Tiny was struck by its quiet, cosy feel. Slightly to the right of the front door was a narrow staircase with a vicious ninety-degree twist at the top. To the left was the drawing room with an open fireplace, and just beyond, towards the rear of the house, a surprisingly spacious kitchen. Rawlings beckoned Tiny through to the kitchen where tea was quickly prepared. It was a delightful room, laid with flagstones, and with a small cream Rayburn set into the old chimney where once an open fire had featured. A raw oak table was set in the centre of the room surrounded by four semi-matching chairs. Under the window, a porcelain butler sink was set into the worktop, adjoined by a wooden draining board which had clearly been scrubbed for many a year to within an inch of its life; a tin of Vim in the corner the likely culprit. The room was wonderfully warm, and Rawlings's satisfaction with his surroundings was apparent. Tiny felt humbled by the pride Rawlings clearly had for such simplicity.

As they sat, Rawlings poured the tea whilst Tiny apologised for his late arrival and recounted his experience daring to use the main entrance. Rawlings remained silent. Tiny thought he was being quite reasonable, although Rawlings had experienced on many occasions Tiny's limited tolerance for authority, status and any type of patronising arrogance.

Keen to hear how Tiny was settling into his new home especially after so many years in London, Rawlings turned the conversation toward Bourne House, the village and the local characters. As Tiny described his encounters, Rawlings smiled, mainly at Tiny's naivety about village life. Fortunately for him, he was still regarded as a local, and didn't have to try to fit in. He felt comfortable back in his childhood home, and of course he knew the area and its people well. Saying that, he didn't really know the new owners of the estate, despite living in one of their cottages. Although he had recently undertaken a couple of small maintenance jobs, it was mainly for the mistress of the house rather than for the main man.

The owners of the estate were Pam and Chuck Stern, an interesting couple who seemed to know less about the equestrian 'sport of kings' than Tiny. Rawlings reported that Pam appeared to be quite friendly, and although now in her late forties, she had a youthful elegance with a figure that disguised her years. Rawlings couldn't help but emphasise how much attention she paid to her appearance, much to Tiny's embarrassment. Even when she dressed casually, Rawlings reported that Pam always took care of the way she looked and was never seen without make-up. Chuck on the other hand was somewhat different, and not someone Rawlings instinctively warmed to. Brash and loud, Chuck acted as if he owned all he surveyed – including the people, whether they were employed by him or not. Falling somewhere between a Texas cowhand and an English squire, Chuck struck an interesting pose. Rawlings was still unsure what he really thought of him. They hadn't fallen out yet, and for the security of his tenancy if nothing else, he was keen to keep it that way.

Sitting comfortably in the kitchen, Tiny and Rawlings continued to chat about this and that. There was however, only one topic that Tiny was really interested in discussing, and he quickly turned the conversation to the death of Stephen Cole. Tiny explained that Stephen's Aunt Margaret cleaned for him, and how upset she was when she heard of the news. He also mentioned that the village of Oakshaw seemed to be talking about little else, including wild speculation about the cause of death.

Rawlings mentioned that initially there had been a moderate police presence, but it had been wound down about a week previously, although matters were a long way from getting back to anything like normal. Although the cordons had now been removed, it wasn't unusual for the occasional police car still to be on site.

"Surely it was just an accident?" Tiny enquired.

"Well, it looks that way, although it was a little odd," Rawlings replied.

"Odd?"

"Well, if anyone knew their horses, it was Stephen. We were all a little surprised when we learnt that he was trampled to death in the stables."

As tea was almost finished, Tiny suggested that perhaps they should have a look at the scene, although he didn't really know what purpose that would serve.

As they left the cottage and walked towards the stable block, a Ford Escort police patrol car was parked across the entrance, and adjacent to it, a dark blue Ford Sierra. Two men were chatting to someone Tiny took to be one of the estate staff. Rawlings explained that the two men from the blue Sierra were policemen, though Tiny had seen more than enough police in his time and had already guessed their profession. The other man was Paul Chipping, the Head Lad who had joined the estate with the new owners. A man in his late sixties, Chipping had a reputation for being short tempered and more than a little grumpy. Having been through a difficult divorce several years earlier, he was forced back to work to pay his ex-wife who apparently, was bleeding him dry, as he liked to tell anyone who would listen, and often those who wouldn't.

As Tiny and Rawlings approached the stable entrance, a uniformed constable moved away from the patrol car and gestured for them to stop. Rawlings explained that he lived on the estate, and reluctantly they were allowed through to the main stable area. No one asked who Tiny was, and no explanation was offered.

As Rawlings showed Tiny the stable where Stephen had met his unfortunate demise, the two policemen moved across to greet them, having finished their conversation with Chipping. They didn't seem best pleased.

"And what do you two clowns think you are doing?" exclaimed the older of the two men; the younger one just smirked.

Rawlings stepped in before Tiny could respond. "I'm George Rawlings, I live on the estate."

"And your friend?" the older man responded sarcastically. Rawlings snapped back "Oh... this is his Honour, Justice Horatio Tiny," with a degree of smugness.

Tiny was usually embarrassed by his full title and Rawlings knew it, but on this occasion, he felt quietly comfortable. The colour drained from the older man's face. "My apologies, your Honour," he responded. "I'm Inspector Stock and this is my sergeant." He gestured towards his colleague. "Niven."

The sergeant nodded, hoping for a personal introduction that never came.

"I'm pleased to meet you, Inspector" Tiny responded, polite but cold.

Inspector Stock was a tall man, standing well above Tiny's five feet eleven. Dressed in a grey suit and dark blue woollen overcoat, he looked every inch a policeman. Tiny assessed his age at around the mid-forties, although he always considered guessing a policeman's age was near impossible because of the life most of them seemed to lead. His thick, curly hair was greying slightly, and stress lines were beginning to show around his eyes. The blood vessels across his nose were tinged with red, and this and the nicotine yellowing of his index and middle finger seemed to confirm an unhealthy lifestyle. Sergeant Niven looked worse. Semi-unshaven and wearing a crumpled shirt, the knot of his tie fell an inch or two below his open top button, His near vagrant appearance was completed by a well-worn olive-green waterproof coat. A little shorter than his inspector, though broader, heavier and sporting a protruding belly, it was clear that he and good health were unfamiliar bedfellows. Although he was probably five or so years younger than Inspector Stock, Sergeant Niven's hair was thin and barely covered his balding scalp.

"Can I help you, sir?" Inspector Stock enquired.

A conversation ensued, in which details were exchanged about Tiny's connection to Stephen and the circumstances surrounding the incident that resulted in Stephen's unfortunate death. It transpired that the horse was so distressed during and following the incident that it had to be destroyed.

Tiny was puzzled.

"Did we determine why the horse was so distressed?" he enquired. "I assume a post mortem was conducted?" Tiny added.

An embarrassing pause ensued.

"I'm sorry, sir, can I just clarify your interest here?" The inspector responded defensively.

"Just a concerned citizen, that's all" Tiny assured him.

"In that case, if you don't mind, sir, there's no need to worry, we have matters in hand." Inspector Stock added trying hard to close down the conversation.

"I'm sure you have," Tiny unconvincingly assured him, "however I was just wondering..."

"I'm sorry sir, we really have to be going." With that the inspector bade Tiny and Rawlings farewell, and walked back to the Sierra closely followed by his sergeant. A short while later, and with the patrol car following, they were gone.

"Gives you a warm glow of confidence, doesn't it?" Tiny observed sardonically.

Rawlings smiled. "I think the horse was a little more than distressed," he replied. "Apparently it went bonkers!"

"I wouldn't mind knowing the outcome of the post mortem," Tiny responded thoughtfully, "just for interest, you understand."

"Inspector Stock didn't confirm there was one," Rawlings pointed out.

"There will be now." Tiny smiled, and turned back towards his car.

Before he could reach his Morgan, Paul Chipping, limping rather distinctively, came scurrying across the yard on an obvious intercept course. Wearing a tweed shooting jacket and green Hunter wellington boots, his full head of long white hair protruded rather bizarrely from the moleskin cap perched on his head

"I say... you there!" His voice echoed around the yard.

Tiny paused, and slowly turned. Putting on his best smile, to disguise his growing irritation, he greeted the man. "Good morning; Mr Chipping, I believe? I was just visiting my friend, Mr Rawlings….." Tiny was prevented from finishing his sentence.

"You have no business being in the yard!" Paul Chipping responded with a show of arrogance which Tiny didn't rise to.

"Well, I'm leaving now, so there's no problem." Tiny responded as he opened the door of his Morgan. Rawlings stayed quiet, standing by the gate of his cottage, embarrassed but unable to intervene.

"You need my permission to be in the yard – that's something you might like to remember," Chipping added with a growing degree of pomposity.

"I'll give you a call later," Tiny called to Rawlings and in so doing, instantly ceased any further engagement with Paul Chipping.

As Tiny drove away from the Ashbury Estate, he felt uncomfortable. It may have been the long, lingering glare from Paul Chipping which followed him towards the lane. Maybe it was the hostile reception he had encountered from Inspector Stock and his sergeant, or perhaps it was the unfamiliar environment or just the attitude of everyone involved. Whatever the reason, it made him uneasy. Stephen's death may well have been a tragic accident, but judging by how defensive everyone seemed to be, there appeared to be more to this incident than met the eye. Tiny was naturally suspicious, and this was an itch that was beginning to grow. Besides, he owed it to Margaret, and of course, to Stephen's parents, to find out more.

Chapter Five

After a thoughtful afternoon pondering the events of the day, Tiny telephoned Rawlings. Rather than discussing matters over the telephone, they agreed to meet in the Oakshaw Arms later that evening. Rawlings arrived first and managed to secure a quiet table in the corner farthest away from the bar. It was still early and the pub was quiet, and whilst sometimes a blessing, it's often more private to have a conversation in a busy room where it's a struggle to hear your conversation let alone someone else's.

Tiny arrived around five minutes later at precisely 6.45 pm as agreed. His pedantic obsession with timekeeping annoyed even him, although of course, he would never admit to it especially after failing so miserably earlier in the day.

Rawlings was already enjoying a pint of the Oakshaw Arms Best Bitter, so Tiny collected his bottle of Guinness and joined him at his table. Fortunately, a few more peopled were beginning to arrive including a party of six celebrating a birthday. Never had Tiny been so grateful for a little noise.

"So, Mr Rawlings, what did you make of this morning?" Tiny enquired.

The two old comrades discussed at length the events as they had played out earlier that day, analysing each person's behaviour. Rawlings provided Tiny with the few additional details he knew, although most of the workers at the Ashbury Estate were relatively new.

"Mr Chipping seemed a little excited?" Tiny stated provocatively.

"I'd say! He's never in the best of moods but just lately, he's been particularly grumpy."

"Nasty limp I noticed?"

"Yes, apparently he originally trained as a professionally jockey but some incident on the track with another rider cut short his career."

"That's a shame."

"Happens to a lot of jockeys apparently, but I don't think his divorce a few years ago helps his mood." Rawlings added more with speculation than fact.

The two men quietly sipped their beer, contemplating the situation.

Almost in passing, Rawlings mentioned that the new owners were planning to host a reception for the racing community and local dignitaries.

"Really?" Tiny commented thoughtfully. "It would be interesting to meet the new owners. Who's arranging the guest list?"

"Mrs Stern appears to be in charge." Rawlings commented in a rather assuming sort of way. "All the estate workers and residents have already been invited, although I'm sure it was an afterthought, just to show their friends how charitable they are." he added rather bitterly.

"You shouldn't be ungrateful," Tiny rebuked. "it's kind of them to host a reception and generous to invite the estate residents."

"Do you think you can get me on the guest list?" he asked Rawlings.

"Well, I can ask... No, actually, I'm sure I can, leave it to me," Rawlings added humbly. "I'll speak with Mrs Stern in the morning."

With that the two comrades parted. Rawlings decided to make a discreet exit and left through the rear door to the car park. Tiny bid Tony and the locals farewell and slipped into the darkness for the short walk home to Bourne House.

It was around 10.00 am the next day when the telephone rang. It one of those wet, late spring mornings and Tiny was sitting in his study reading the newspaper.

"Good morning sir, Rawlings here. I've spoken with Mrs Stern, and she would be delighted if you could join them for their evening reception."

"Excellent, thank you, Mr Rawlings, good work. When is it?" Tiny asked.

"Oh, yes, I forgot to mention. It's this Thursday evening, from 7.30 pm."

"...And the dress code?" Tiny enquired.

"Black tie apparently."

Tiny's heart sank. He thought his days of attending black tie events were over. "Won't that be a little awkward for the estate workers?" Tiny enquired.

"Exactly!"

Maybe Rawlings's earlier assumption had been close to the truth after all, Tiny thought.

Thursday evening was fresh and rather blustery as Tiny struggled awkwardly with his black tie. Normally Patricia would have helped him with such paraphernalia, and although initially he didn't really need any assistance, he enjoyed the attention. It had become such a ritual over the years that he had almost forgotten how to dress himself and now when he needed a little help, he was alone. It was the small things that triggered the most poignant memories, he thought to himself as his mind drifted to all the good times they had together.

Arriving at Ashbury Hall a little after 7.45 pm, Tiny parked his Morgan between a new Range Rover and a rather mature Bentley before walking towards the main door. He smiled to himself and wondered if he would once again be directed to the tradesmen's entrance. This time the door was already open and flanked either side by elegant glazed ceramic containers, each housing a pair of bay balls interwoven with twinkly lights. On either side of the entrance stood two hostesses each holding a tray of what he assumed to be champagne. Before Tiny could accept a drink, an elderly man approached from behind and asked if he could take his coat. As he turned to greet him, Tiny smiled broadly.

"I hope you don't mind me using the main entrance?" he asked rather mischievously. The colour drained from the elderly man's face as he silently took Tiny's overcoat and hung it on a long rail on the opposite side of the hall.

As Tiny sipped his champagne, his eyes darted around the interior of the house trying to assess the character of the residents from the style of the decor. It was an odd blend, mainly traditional with the occasional piece of modern artwork dotted around. The hall featured a beautiful parquet floor with oak panelled walls; straight ahead was the main reception room where a crowd was beginning to gather. To the left was a double-width, one eighty-degree staircase featuring quarter landings, again constructed from seasoned oak. As Tiny wandered along the hall towards the main reception room, he noticed a modern polished metal sculpture with a hole in its centre, mounted on a plinth. It was a sizeable piece, and clearly there to make a statement although exactly what it was stating Tiny wasn't sure.

As he entered the reception room, he was forced to brush past a group of guests stood in the doorway. Tiny never understood why people seemed to be drawn to doorways, especially as they were constantly being asked to move. As the group once again filled the void Tiny left in his wake, he caught glimpse of Rawlings talking to an attractive middle-aged lady. As he approached, Rawlings turned and with a smile made the first introduction of the evening.

"Hello, sir. Can I introduce you to Mrs Stern."

Pam Stern greeted Tiny with a warm smile. A fashion model in her younger years, Pam was an elegant and slim lady, and though now in her late forties, she still carried herself with youthful grace. Conservatively dressed in a long figure-hugging evening gown, and wearing ostentatious jewellery with ease, it was clear than here was a woman who was used to the finer things in life. Although her blonde hair denied the obvious undertones of grey, Tiny thought Pam Stern cut quite a dash.

"I'm very pleased to meet you, Mrs Stern. I'm…"

Before Tiny could finish his sentence, Mrs Stern interrupted.

"Oh please call me Pam. I've heard so much about you. Chuck and I are so pleased you could join our little soirée this evening…" Pam continued talking for several minutes without pausing for breath. She waxed lyrical about how wonderful she and Chuck thought England was, (no argument there Tiny thought to himself) and how she just loved the Ashbury Estate. Pam was just beginning to talk about her love of all matters equestrian when a larger than life character, who previously had been deep in conversation with a group of business men huddled near one of the bay windows, caught sight of them and approached with purpose.

"Hey, you must be Sir Horatio," Chuck announced in a booming voice. "Pleased to make your acquaintance, sir."

Someone has been doing his research Tiny thought with a smile. "Please, just Tiny; I gave up all that formality when I left London," he responded, a little embarrassed.

Chuck was probably in his mid-sixties, with snow-white hair and a well-trimmed moustache to match. As a short but rather broad fellow, he could best be described as 'solid'. Dressed in a tailored evening suit he had a sort of presence that Tiny admired.

"What brought you to England?" Tiny enquired, trying hard to move the conversation along.

As Tiny engaged in small talk, Rawlings was noticeably sidelined. Both Chuck and Pam were focused on Tiny and were clearly doing their utmost to make a new friend. Tiny was wary and felt slightly sorry for Rawlings. Trying not to be being too obvious, Tiny turned the conversation to the demise of Stephen.

"That was just terrible." Pam exclaimed.

Chuck's manner changed, and adopting a more serious tone he added,

"It's actually really bad for business too. People are beginning to talk, and the police, my goodness, will they ever leave us alone?" Chuck uttered trying hard to make it sound like he was whispering.

Perhaps Tiny shouldn't have been surprised by their practical approach; maybe they didn't know Stephen too well. All the same, he was taken aback by their lack of sensitivity.

Tiny gently probed to see if there was any clue as to why the horse reacted so aggressively. He asked about the horses' normal routine and learnt the Ashbury Estate had a total of fourteen. The business had recently merged with a similar set-up in Ireland with horses regularly travelling from over from the stables located just outside Galway.

"A friend of mine, Eben Weller, known him for years, was keen to get in on the British scene and asked me to look after some of his horses," Chuck continued. "South African chap, nice fellow." He added.

"Is Mr Weller in the same line of business?" Tiny enquired. Of course, what he really wanted to know was how Chuck made his money.

"Well, sort of…" Chuck said hesitantly. "Eben's in media and needs my technology to make it happen!" He added with a booming laugh, "My guys are getting into this new satellite business. It's the future of broadcasting, you mark my words." He stated confidently.

It transpired that Chuck had originally manufactured equipment for cable media but had recently become involved in the world of satellites. Working with a couple of British companies, Chuck was spending so much time in the UK he decided to purchase a property, hence the Ashbury Estate.

"Hey Tiny, are you into horse racing?" Chuck enquired.

"Well…" Tiny started to respond but didn't get very far.

"Of course you are," Chuck exclaimed excitedly, placing a vice-like hand on Tiny's shoulder. "All you Brits love that sort of thing. Take the Grand National, it's an institution, am I right?" Chuck exclaimed rhetorically.

"I tell you what." he continued. "Why don't you come down to Newbury races with us next week? As our guest of course."

Tiny was taken aback. "Umm... well, yes..." Before Tiny could finish his sentence, Chuck chipped in, "That's settles it. Rawlings can let you have all the details. In fact, why doesn't Rawlings come with you? Make a day of it for you both."

Tiny wasn't quite sure what Chuck meant, but he was grateful that his old colleague hadn't been forgotten.

Pam glanced at Tiny, smiled seductively, but said nothing.

Niceties complete, Chuck and Pam made their apologies and, being the perfect hosts, moved politely on to their next target. In one way, Tiny was relieved; in another, disappointed. He had enjoyed their company, especially Pam's elegance, and revelled in Chuck's charisma, which he admired and unconsciously envied.

After a minute or so of silence, Rawlings felt the need to say something. "Well, that was Chuck and Pam," he stated rather obviously.

Tiny ignored the platitudinous remark. He had spotted Inspector Stock looking rather uncomfortable in the far corner of the room. As Tiny approached, with Rawlings in tow, he noticed the inspector clutching a glass of brown ale.

"No champagne, Inspector?" he enquired. Without leaving time for a reply, he added rather mischievously "On duty I suppose?"

"No, I'm not. I just can't stand the stuff," came the response. "I thought you would be here," he added rather sarcastically.

"Nice suit, very smart," Tiny lied, smiling broadly whilst staring at the ill-fitting dinner suit that hung awkwardly from the inspector's frame. "How's the investigation coming along?" Tiny enquired, trying hard to move the conversation on rather than getting drawn into a tit-for-tat conversation that wasn't going to end well for either party.

"What investigation? I told you it was an accident," Inspector Stock insisted. "There's nothing to investigate," he added with a sense of finality.

"So, no post mortem on the horse?"

"Ah, well, no..."

"No?"

"By the time we asked, it was too late. The horse had already, well, you know, been 'processed'." The inspector replied rather sheepishly.

Rawlings, rather unsubtly, raised his eyebrows.

"Well, as you say, it was probably just an accident., Tiny concluded charitably. "It was good to meet you again, inspector." He added trying to close down the conversation to which, the Inspector was happy to oblige.

After exchanging farewell pleasantries with the inspector, Tiny and Rawlings continued to circle the room in an attempt to work their way towards the door. By pure luck, or perhaps unavoidable fate, Paul Chipping was entering the room with a small, weaselly man, just as Tiny and Rawlings was trying to exit.

Tiny took the initiative. "Mr Chipping, how nice it is to see you again."

"Oh, yes... it's Mr Tiny, isn't it?"

"Just call me Tiny."

"I think we make have got off on the wrong foot earlier in the week," Chipping added apologetically.

"Did we? I can't recall," Tiny lied diplomatically.

"Can I introduce Joe Harrison, the estate's assistant trainer," Chipping announced in an obvious attempt to deflect attention away from himself. Joe grinned like a child and held out a clammy hand, which thankfully Rawlings stepped in and decided to shake. Tiny judged Joe to be around thirty-five years old although it was apparent that he had endured a hard life. He was a small skinny man with a protruding belly, thinning hair and a scruffy, ill-kept beard. His interpretation of a dinner suit showed an obvious effort to look 'modern' however quality was a concept which had completely bypassed this young man.

The conversation continued awkwardly. Joe kept quiet, nursing his now warm glass of champagne and grinning like a sinister imbecile. Paul Chipping shifted from foot to foot betraying his cool persona, his every word carefully measured. Obviously, he now knew who Tiny was, and unlike their first encounter, he displayed uncharacteristic humility. What he couldn't work out was why Tiny was so interested in the accident and what connection he had with Stephen. Before he could enquire further, a younger, more dynamic man arrived and joined the conversation.

"Good evening, Mr Tiny. I'm Ian Parkinson, Mr Stern's trainer and stud manager."

Paul Chipping fell profoundly silent and retreated into the background. Joe stood his ground but remained quiet.

"Please, just Tiny. It's good to meet you."

Tiny judged Ian Parkinson to be around forty-five years old. He was an average height, slim(ish) man with a square jaw and jet-black hair swept back and obviously held in place using some kind of product. Here was a man who cared about his appearance and knew how to dress.

"How long have you been at the Ashbury Estate?" Tiny enquired.

"Not long – about two years," Parkinson responded. "I used to manage a yard in Jo'burg."

"I thought I detected a slight accent," Tiny responded. "Is Johannesburg your home?"

"Not really, although I was there for quite a few years."

"What brought you to the UK?"

"I wanted to expand into the international market, and as I used to train for Eben Weller, it was a natural move."

"Eben Weller?" Tiny enquired, more surprised than inquisitive.

"He's a friend of Mr Stern and the owner of several horses and a training yard in Galway. That's in Ireland, you know."

Tiny knew.

"When I recently decided to move to the UK, Mr Weller kindly persuaded Mr Stern to let me take over the yard here," Parkinson added proudly.

"Well, you've certainly had an impact." Tiny politely commented. "I've heard you've had a significant degree of success."

"It's a team effort," Parkinson responded with false modesty. "Paul and my assistant Joe must share most of the credit."

As the conversation progressed, Tiny discovered that the main yard was actually based in Galway, and the Ashbury Estate was more of a secondary hub. During the UK season, however, they mainly used the stables on the Ashbury Estate, especially when racing internationally. Tiny found this quite surprising not realising, perhaps naively, that horse racing was such a global affair. Apart from races in Ireland, England and mainland Europe, racing in the Middle East, Hong Kong, America and even as far as Australia was commonplace for some yards, although not yet for the Ashbury Estate.

Tiny was fascinated to learn that some horses still travelled by sea, but recently air travel was becoming more popular. Traveling by air involved a separate freight aircraft, with each horse accompanied by a certified 'flying groom' specially qualified to manage the animal's in-flight needs. Tiny was impressed by how well they were cared for, a bit different from PanAm economy class, he thought to himself.

Continuing Tiny's education, Ian mentioned the strict quarantine regulations that had to be taken into consideration. Although these varied from country to country, they often involved time spent in isolation.

Tiny's interest in race horses was growing by the minute, but he had little to add to the conversation.

Thinking on his feet, he proudly announced, "Mr Rawlings and I will be joining Chuck and Pam next week at Newbury races."

"You will?" Chipping suddenly interjected, failing miserably to disguise his surprise.

"That's great news," Ian responded, scowling at Chipping. "It's a lovely course and a good day out. I'm pleased you can come along."

Tiny was getting tired and decided it was time to move on. "I'm sure we will see you both there," He politely added before bidding Parkinson and Chipping farewell.

The rest of the evening was fairly uneventful. Tiny had achieved his mission and was now looking to leave as soon as possible. Despite years of painful practice, parties still made him feel awkward. All the same, he was impressed by the whole event, and not in any small way by Pam. He secretly looked forward to his trip to Newbury races although he had no idea what to expect. Maybe that's what he found exciting. He hadn't been to the races before but was beginning to get a taste for this new aristocratic lifestyle.

Chapter Six

As the day of Newbury races dawned, Tiny felt a twinge of regret that he had embraced the invitation extended by Chuck and Pam, with such enthusiasm. He wasn't sure whether to blame the heady aristocratic atmosphere of Ashbury Hall or the champagne which he did admit, had been generously poured. Either way, he would have been grateful for an excuse not to attend. "Why, oh why, did I agree?" he exclaimed to the empty house. "I would much rather have a day in the garden. And what do I wear to such an event?" He thought to himself.

As his attention dwelled upon plausible reasons not to leave the house, the telephone rang.

"Good morning, sir, Rawlings here. As we are both off to Newbury today, I was wondering if you would like me to drive you?"

Any possibility of an excuse not to attend suddenly evaporated. He couldn't deny Rawlings his day out.

"That's a very kind offer, Mr Rawlings, thank you. It would be greatly appreciated."

At 11.00 am on the button, the doorbell rang. Already in the hall deciding which shoes to wear, Tiny immediately opened the front door to find Rawlings smiling. Tiny rather unsubtly looked him up and down with a frown that grew stronger as Rawlings tipped his hat. The chocolate coloured fedora accompanied a camel hair overcoat which being unbuttoned, allowed the olive green tweed suit underneath to peak out. Rawlings's outfit was a festival of colour, and a little to 'busy' for Tiny's taste. In contrast, Rawlings looked at Tiny's rather dull sports jacket, checked shirt and corduroy trousers with surprise and was about to utter that he would wait for Tiny to change but thought better of it. Tiny, on the other hand was thinking about second-hand car salesmen, but like Rawlings, also kept his thoughts to himself.

"Ready when you are sir." Rawlings added, maintaining his smile.

"Thank you, Mr Rawlings. Here are the keys; I don't suppose you could bring the Morgan around the front?"

Despite the promise of summer trying hard to drive spring away for yet another year, the grass was wet after several days of rain. Tiny was thinking how easy it would be to turn a grass field into a slippery mud bath. Ever practical, Tiny tried hard to ensure he was prepared and so chose his sturdiest pair of waterproof shoes.

Soon they were off, although disappointingly it was a little too cool to lower the hood on the Morgan. Tiny quite enjoyed driving short journeys, but he was just as happy being driven and was grateful for Rawlings's offer, especially as he didn't know the area very well.

The journey was no more than forty minutes, and upon entering Newbury, Rawlings took a detour away from the signed route to car park 1. "You don't want to follow the recommended directions?" Tiny enquired, a little worried.

"Apparently car park 1 is in the centre of the course and can get really muddy," came the reply. "Car park 2 is far better; and besides, it's exclusively for the owners and trainers, and as we have our blue badges..." Rawlings added with confidence.

Tiny was quietly impressed, but said nothing.

No sooner had Rawlings locked the car, Tiny noticed Chuck's striking figure striding across the grass to greet them. Dressed in a short sheepskin coat, his stature oozed confidence.

'Glad you could make it. We are just having a few drinks. I'll introduce you to the team." Chuck extended his arms and with a movement that left little choice, ushered both Tiny and Rawlings towards the hospitality area on the upper levels of the main grandstand.

Tiny's heart sank. I suppose I shouldn't be surprised, he thought; after all, racing is all about fun, enjoyment and entertainment. The fact however remained, the older Tiny became the less he enjoyed the social aspect of life. He used to feel obliged to make an effort, and felt a little left out if he wasn't included, but that had faded years ago and he no longer felt the need to pretend. All the same, he knew that if he wanted to find out more about the death of Stephen, he needed to be in the mix.

56

Wearing his best smile, Tiny diligently followed Chuck's lead, although secretly he was desperate to have a look around on his own.

Upon reaching the owners' suite on the top floor of the hospitality area, Tiny politely took the time to shake the hands of all the members of the team, well, the ones who were there and not downstairs somewhere busying themselves with the horses. There were several other guests including a couple of the senior lads, along with Joe Harrison, Ian Parkinson and of course Pam and Chuck. Once again, Tiny was struck by Pam's elegance. Dressed beautifully in a high neck cream embroidered blouse, tweed skirt and matching jacket, her presence lit up the room.

Dragging his eyes away from Pam, Tiny was impressed by the opulence of his surroundings and by the facilities on offer. Just to the rear of the main grandstand was the parade ring where, according to Rawlings, the horses were displayed prior to the race. In the centre of the ring Tiny could see a small podium surrounded by advertising hoardings. To one side of the podium, there appeared to be a television crew busying themselves with lights and an endless number of wires. The parade ring, he later discovered, doubled as the presentation area after each race for the winners along with interviews and photographs for the owners and trainers. Tiny excused himself from the group and decided to sneak away and have a quick look around. Beyond the parade ring were two buildings of similar size which Tiny later discovered accommodated those who weren't lucky enough to have 'premier' tickets. From the rear, the buildings looked to be all hospitality however as Tiny rounded the corner he saw that the front was actually a grandstand and was open to the elements. There were several tiers with the lower section accommodating a standing area which was partitioned into sections by crush barriers. The seating available in the upper tiers appeared to be far more popular as the crowd gathered in preparation for the race ahead. A large cantilevered roof, designed to keep the worst of the elements at bay, completed these most impressive buildings. Looking towards the track, Tiny noticed a narrow strip of grass that was rapidly filling up with people, or as Rawlings would so aptly describe as punters.

As Tiny started to make his way back to his own party he was fascinated by the on-course betting stands and the obviously meaningful gestures the bookies were exchanging. Their stands consisted of little more than a wooden box and a chalkboard on a stick, however Tiny could see the fistful of notes each 'turf accountant' was holding. Most were wearing woollen overcoats accompanied by either a trilby or coke hat. Without exception, they were all feverishly busy gathering cash, while their assistants constantly rubbed out and rewrote the odds of each horse as trading ebbed and flowed. Tiny found this fascinating, and was riveted to the spot as he soaked up the atmosphere.

Not being a gambler, and having little clue what separated one horse from another, Tiny kept his hands firmly in his pocket. His sensible side was saying there were far better ways of wasting money, but the atmosphere was starting to get to him, and he secretly began to fancy a little flutter.

By the time he arrived back at the hospitality suite, most of the group had already moved over to the parade ring for the first race. Towards the back of the room Rawlings was chatting, a little too intently, to one of the female guests. She seemed relieved when Tiny attracted Rawlings's attention and took the opportunity to discreetly slip away.

"Oh hello, sir," Rawlings muttered, with a little embarrassment.

"We are supposed to be having a look around...to find out more about their operation," Tiny reminded him with a hint of sarcasm. "Or have you forgotten about poor Stephen?" Tiny rebuked trying to muster up a little sympathy.

"Sorry sir, however I did find out from Samantha, one of the stable staff, that the horse that killed Stephen had recently been sent over from Galway and was unsettled for a couple of days before the incident."

Tiny felt a little guilty for being so harsh, but tried hard not to show it.

"They seem to be getting the horses ready for the first race," Tiny commented trying to change to subject, "Let's move over to the parade ring."

"It's a little late for that sir, the runners for the first race are already on their way out," Rawlings replied. "We can watch this first race from here if you like?"

Tiny was a little disappointed, but equally impressed that matters were moving on so quickly. Stood by the windows of the owners' hospitality area, Tiny had a great view albeit from quite a distance from the action. Although he enjoyed privileged surroundings, he yearned to be down among the punters, experiencing the atmosphere.

Chuck and Pam returned just as the race was starting, together with a clique of very jovial guests whose laughter seemed to more than fill the room. As Tiny politely sipped his second glass of champagne, trying hard to blend in with the wallpaper, the first race was over. Determined not to miss the second, Tiny signalled to Rawlings and together, they made their way downstairs. This early in the season, everything looked immaculate and polished to within an inch of its life. Upon reaching the parade ring, Tiny and Rawlings leant against the freshly painted white wooden rail which separated the public from the horses. The grass in the centre looked like carpet; the ring around the outside was laid with fresh bark, creating a soft, safe and hazard free track for the horses to parade with pride. As the runners for the second race began to gather, a groom led each horse around while over the public address system, facts and figures were announced about each of their various achievements. The parade was an example of equine perfection. Each horse, although lively, was beautifully toned and glistened in the early spring sunshine. The Ashbury Estate had two horses running that day, The Bishop, which was apparently due to run later, and Choirboy, which was making its debut in the second race. Tiny was intrigued by the intricate names associated with all the horses and wondered if the ecclesiastical references to the two horses from the Ashbury Estate were mere coincidence or perhaps, had any deeper meaning.

As Tiny pondered thoughtfully, the jockeys appeared. He was surprised by just how small they were, which seemed even more evident when they stood beside a horse. He watched in fascination as the jockeys strolled around, chatting to various dignitaries before a bell rang, and they joined their mounts and began to saddle up. Tiny was amazed by just how delicate and flimsy the saddles were which seemed to be more akin to an A4 pad of paper than an actual saddle. Within moments, the jockeys began to take charge as the lads began to lead the horses out of the ring and towards the course. The Choirboy seemed to be livelier than most, and was proving more than a handful for the obviously competent jockey.

"He seems to want to run!" Rawlings exclaimed.

"Isn't that the point?" Tiny replied rather impatiently.

As if the tide had suddenly turned, the crowd melted away from the parade ring and drifted towards the grandstand and trackside with the greatest concentration not surprisingly, being near the finish line. The tic-tac 'turf accountants' were reaching fever pitch as small crowds gathered around each one desperate to be relieved of their money. Rather than joining Chuck, Pam and the other invitees in the owners' box, Tiny decided to mix with the crowd and experience the event from the trackside. After all, there was only so much champagne and small talk he could cope with.

Together with Rawlings, he moved with the mass of people towards the front of the grandstand. It was clear that Rawlings was eyeing up the odds from each of the bookies on-route. "Choirboy is four to one," he commented. "Shall we have a fiver on the nose?"

Tiny turned to his companion with a puzzled, slightly disapproving look. "A fiver?" he asked. "It's up to you of course, but if you are going to be reckless, I suppose you could put a pound on for me." He added passing one of the new one-pound coins across to Rawlings. Tiny still couldn't get used to a coin being a pound, and didn't really regard it as money. This eased his mind a little, although he had no idea why he felt so guilty, maybe it was because secretly he also felt quite excited.

With a wry smile Rawlings took the pound coin, and disappeared into the crowd. Within minutes, he was back with two slips of papers covered with incomprehensible scribbles. "Here you are, sir, your slip. I managed to get nine to two on Devonshire Lad, so that's where my fiver is; I heard a tip as I waited in the queue," he announced proudly.

Tiny just frowned in dismay and said nothing as they walked towards the edge of the track. The area around the finishing line was already crowded so they moved a little further along to ensure they could see the action.

The deafening public address system was updating the crowd, and probably half of Newbury town, on the progress of the 'runners and riders' as they made their way along the edge of the course towards the starting gate. As Tiny surveyed the crowd, he noticed a sea of binoculars watching the horses every move. For some bizarre reason, this seemed to only add to the excitement.

The start seemed to take forever, and Tiny was becoming impatient as the marshals tried hard to encourage the last few horses into the starting gates. Choirboy appeared to be putting up the most resistance, although without binoculars, Tiny had to rely upon the running commentary for updates. The atmosphere near the finishing line was distinctly tense as finally the announcement of 'They're under starters orders' echoed around the grandstand. After a short couple of seconds, a ripple of relief seemed to run through the crowd as 'They're off!' was announced with more than a little excitement.

As the crowd strained to see the early leaders the announcer on the public address system went into overdrive with an almost incomprehensible rhythmic commentary, which to non-equine enthusiasts, sounded like concealed code.

Tiny was surprised by the urgency of it all, which considering it was a race, shouldn't have come as a shock. What he did find most unusual was the amount of pushing and shoving which seemed to be going on amongst the horses and riders. Although others were involved, the main culprit appeared to be Choirboy, who being near the middle, seemed to be causing a considerable nuisance to the other riders. As they approached the first hurdle there was a faller; it was Devonshire Lad. Horse and rider seemed OK, although Rawlings's face fell in disappointment. Tiny tried hard not to smirk.

As the pack turned the corner for home the tension began to intensify. The advancing posse of horses seemed to grow larger as they drew closer to the finish line. The thunder of hooves although steadily increasing, was almost drowned out by the cheering crowd. Progress could be felt through vibrations deep in the ground as twelve supercharged athletic thoroughbreds pounded the turf in unison. My goodness, Tiny thought to himself, as a feeling of nervousness was replaced with a slight sense of fear. The pushing and shoving on the track continued and was beginning to cause concern. Over another jump and then another. All the horses were still running, though it was clear that a further two had lost their jockeys. As the pushing and shoving became more extreme, the finishing line drew closer. A slight sense of anxiety was now starting to become detectable in the commentator's voice as the trackside marshals looked around in dismay, not quite sure what, if anything, they should do.

The horses loomed large as they steadily approached the finish line. Just one more jump to master and then the sprint for home. The jockey on board Choirboy was obviously struggling to maintain control with the animal constantly moving from side to side. With the final jump behind them, and another jockey lost, the finish line was suddenly within touching distance. Tiny strained to see over the heads of the crowd who had massed against the finish post whilst Rawlings had disappeared into the throng of excited supporters.

Tiny didn't really see what happened next but a mighty crash was followed by screaming. He remained glued to the spot unable to move as he watched panic ensue. The crowd, which only moments ago had been alive with excitement, were now running from the trackside in fear. Sobbing, gasping, cries and swearing could be heard all around.

As the people dispersed, Tiny could begin to see the scene. Half a dozen people lay on the grass around a gaping gap in the fence. A horse was lying on its side amongst the fallen people, its legs thrashing wildly. It was obviously trying to get on to its feet but with no success. Tiny was struck by its glazed staring eyes which clearly revealed its distress, fear and confusion. Although Tiny was fearful of the damage a wounded horse could do to injured people lying so close, still he could not move. He caught a brief glimpse of what appeared to be the jockey, who was lying motionless on the far side of the horse. He feared the worst, but remained glued to the spot, trying hard to make sense of the events stretching out before him.

As he struggled to mentally process the distressing sight of the carnage, panic and fear, two marshals ran towards the scene as sirens began to drown out the screams. All the other horses had disappeared as if they had never existed. When the marshals reached the scene, one held the head of the fallen horse flat on the grass to prevent it from trying to get up, whilst the other started to tend to the injured. As people vacated the area, Tiny could see more clearly. He gasped when he realised the horse was Choirboy.

As the first ambulance arrived, Tiny regained his senses and moved back a little. He felt guilty that he had not done anything to help, but he was still struggling to take in what was happening. Other marshals arrived with a policeman and together, began to move people away from the area. The medical team started to treat the injured as more marshals arrived and took control of the growing voyeuristic crowd now eager to see what was happening. As Tiny walked back towards the grandstand in shock, a second ambulance crew joined their colleagues.

"Sir, sir!" a voice cried out. It was Rawlings. "Are you all right, sir? I lost you in the crowd."

Tiny didn't reply.

As the two comrades moved into the grandstand the gasps of shock and horror from the crowd were overwhelming. As they made their way towards the hospitality area, they were greeted by Chuck who was running down the stairs.

"Oh my goodness!" he exclaimed. "It's Choirboy!" He added as he disappeared into the advancing crowd. Pam was a few feet behind, but paused when she met Tiny. Neither spoke for a moment. Tiny glanced into her tear-filled eyes and instinctively reached for her hand. With a little squeeze he broke the silence, "Why don't you stay with us. You really don't want to go down there," he said gently.

Pam smiled weakly and without question, turned and followed Tiny and Rawlings back into the hospitality area.

All around the racecourse, people were dashing here and there. Pandemonium ensued; no one seemed to know what to do. When they reached the hospitality area Tiny sat Pam down and asked Rawlings to fetch her a glass of water. The atmosphere had completely changed. No longer was fun and laughter the order of the day. The air was now understandably tense with several guests stood alone, deep in thought, while others sat with their heads in their hands.

As Tiny awaited Rawlings's return, an announcement came over the public address system to say that the remainder of the day's races were cancelled. This was swiftly followed by a request to clear the course, Simultaneously the marshals started to usher people towards the car parks. With Pam now settled, Tiny decided to take a look from the balcony to assess the situation. Looking down on the scene that stretched beneath him, it was clear that the emergency services, together with the marshals, had matters under control. Less than ten minutes earlier the air had been filled with excitement and joy, but now a subdued, almost business-like atmosphere prevailed. The area where Choirboy had broken through the rails was cordoned off with red and white striped tape. A pale blue plastic sheet was lying over what Tiny assumed must be a fatality, and a team from each of the two ambulances worked on two further victims. Tiny knew the incident was serious, but was shocked by just how quickly excitement and elation had turned to tragedy. The police were now very much in charge, and were helping the marshals to move onlookers away from the scene.

Tiny suddenly realised that something was missing. Choirboy was gone. As reality began to sink in, he heard raised voices behind him. Turning back to the hospitality area, he found Chuck in the middle of the room making an announcement.

"Friends, please... I have news," he started. "The police have asked if we can make our way to the car park as the rest of the meeting has been cancelled. I don't have any information on the injuries, but I'm pleased to report that though Choirboy is hurt, he's OK." There was relief in his voice as he finished his announcement yet sustained shock and worry were still evident.

As Tiny moved towards Pam, Chuck intercepted him.

"Tiny? Could I ask you an enormous favour? I'm going to be here for a while, and I was wondering if you could escort Pam home for me?"

"Of course, Chuck, I would be happy to," Tiny responded, without thinking about Rawlings and the fact that his Morgan only had two seats.

As everyone filed out of the owners' hospitality suite, they were joined by guests from neighbouring suites slowly making their way downstairs. Tiny caught sight of Rawlings pushing through the crowd towards the door. As he approached from behind, he put his hand on his shoulder and whispered in his ear, "I've just been speaking with Chuck and he's asked if we can ensure Pam gets home safely." After a brief pause, he added, "I think she's still in shock." hoping for a little sympathy.

"But how are we going to..." Rawlings didn't have the chance to finish his sentence.

"I was wondering if you could take the Morgan and meet us back at the Ashbury Estate whilst I arrange a lift in one of the estate's cars? Perhaps arrange to take one of the grooms?" Rawlings looked puzzled. "To see what you can find out?" Tiny whispered.

A plan was hatched.

"Oh, before you leave, you will need this." Tiny added as he handed Rawlings his betting slip. Rawlings looked puzzled again. "Well, Choirboy didn't finish, so I should get my pound back?" Tiny asked rhetorically.

As Rawlings accepted the slip with a slight raising of his eyebrows, he couldn't quite decide what surprised him the most, Tiny's focus on his pound during these dramatic events, or his unexpected knowledge of the gambling rules.

As they reached the bottom of the stairs and exited into the open, the bracing air filled their lungs. In all the excitement and ensuing panic, Tiny had completely forgotten how cold it was however with a little shiver and a rub of his hands Tiny tried to compose himself. As people split into groups, all heading in different directions, Tiny and Rawlings followed the Ashbury Estate team towards to the stables and grooms' area. Shock and tears spread through the group as news emerged that the jockey riding Choirboy had died in the accident. As the news spread to neighbouring yards, grief ensued.

Tiny and Rawlings just looked at each other. They were obviously outsiders in this close-knit community and were very conscious not to intrude. Just as they were feeling rather awkward, and wondering what to do, Tiny caught sight of Ian Parkinson. Quickly bidding farewell to Rawlings, Tiny headed towards Ian, who was surrounded by his team.

"Now listen up everyone. I know we are all upset, but we have a job to do," the stud manager announced with authority. "We need to gather our things and pack them into the trailers. Once the vet has finished with Choirboy, we need to load him and The Bishop and get them both back to the yard pronto. Concentrate people, we need to stay focused!" He concluded with a clap of his hands.

As the group dispersed, Tiny caught Ian's attention. He explained Chuck's request, and detecting the stress in Ian's voice, offered his help. Ian was anxious to check on the vet's progress with Choirboy, and without waiting for an invitation, Tiny accompanied him towards the stables. Pam was speaking with Paul Chipping and didn't seem in any hurry to leave.

As Ian reached the stable, Tiny was about two paces behind. The veterinary team were starting to pack away their equipment as two lads from the Ashbury Estate resumed responsibility for Choirboy. It was clear the horse was still in considerable distress. A large dressing covered a substantial wound on his right shoulder, presumably caused by breaking through the rail. Ian stretched out his hand and placed it gently on Choirboy's nose. It was a tender and calming gesture which in an atmosphere of such stress and tension surprised Tiny.

"Easy, lad..." Ian whispered. "Easy..."

Tiny watched with fascination. The connection Ian had with Choirboy was remarkable. The relationship between the two was obviously special; it was something Tiny had never encountered before. It was more than mere communication; there was a sense of trust, mutual respect and perhaps even love. Tiny was moved.

Choirboy had settled down considerably, although his agitation was still apparent.

"We've patched him up as best we can." The vet said, packing his last few instruments into his bag. "The officials needed a blood sample which we have taken, and here's part of the sample for you." The vet added handing Ian a box containing a phial. "Of course, there will need to be a full enquiry," he added as he walked away from the stable.

"Talk about stating the obvious," Ian commented quietly and rather sarcastically. Turning around, he looked over Tiny's shoulder. "Where's Paul?" he asked.

"Oh, I think he's with Pam," Tiny stated with a degree of certainly.

"Well, he should be here. He's the Head Lad, why the hell isn't he here?"

Tiny judged this to be a rhetorical question and decided to remain quiet. As Ian walked off, Tiny decided it was time to find Pam and arrange to return her to the Ashbury Estate.

Arriving back at the Estate, Tiny noticed his beloved Morgan parked outside the main stable block. Neither Rawlings nor the horse box containing both Choirboy and The Bishop was anywhere to be seen.

As Pam got out of the car, Tiny suggested a cup of tea. Pam smiled with a sense of submission and gently nodded. Tiny tenderly placed his hand on the small of her back and guided her towards the house. "Come on" he said, "there's nothing you can do here."

As they walked towards the house, Tiny noticed Rawlings coming out of one of the stables with Joe Harrison and a couple of the lads he recognised from earlier. Rawlings caught Tiny's eye and with a barely noticeable nod, they continued unabated.

As Tiny entered the house, a sense of calm came over Pam. It was obvious that she was pleased to be home. As they sat at the kitchen table, Tiny busied himself making tea. "There you are." he said, putting a cup in front of her. "There are few problems that aren't improved by a cup of tea." He added reassuringly

Pam smiled endearingly. "It's been such a dreadful day," she sniffed, holding back a tear. "that poor jockey... and the others that were injured." She hastily added.

As they drank their tea and chatted, Pam began to relax. She described her childhood in South Africa, and how she struggled as a fashion model before meeting Chuck. It was clear to Tiny that her grace and elegance hid a difficult and tempestuous youth. Maybe Chuck was her saviour after all, Tiny thought.

"You are such a good listener," Pam said lovingly laying her hand on his. As the warmth of her touch surged through Tiny's veins, the hand was suddenly snatched away; the front door slammed and Chuck's booming voice could be heard in the hallway.

As he entered the kitchen, a polite and respectful scene stretched out before him. "Oh, hello Tiny" he announced with a degree of surprise. "Thank you for looking after Pam for me. It's been quite a day." he added with a sense of frustration and vulnerability. As he sat at the table, Tiny tried to squeeze another cup of tea from the pot. Chuck nodded his appreciation of the gesture, but without making a comment, moved towards the Welsh dresser and pulled out a bottle of Bowmore malt. He waved it at Tiny, who politely shook his head.

Chuck started to talk about the day. He explained that the police had taken an initial statement, but he hadn't been much help. He was at a loss to explain the terrible events that had unfolded earlier. Chuck continued and added that during his conversations with the police, they had confirmed that in addition to the death of the jockey, three spectators were also injured, one seriously.

"In all my years, I have never experienced anything like that," Chuck sighed. "I'm at a loss to explain it."

Tiny decided that Pam and Chuck should be left in peace. He had done what was asked of him and felt it was time to make a discreet exit. Making his excuses, and in receipt of sincere thanks from both Pam and Chuck, he bid them farewell.

As Tiny walked towards the yard, the large dark blue horsebox with the gold logo of the Ashbury Estate emblazoned on the side was slowly moving down the drive. It parked in the central area adjacent to the main stable block just as Tiny arrived. Paul Chipping and a couple of other stable lads climbed out of the cab. Chipping glared across at

Tiny but said nothing. He made quite a fuss about opening the rear of the trailer, whilst barking orders at the stable staff. It was clear that Tiny was surplus to requirements and not welcome.

Tiny quickly took the hint. Besides, he didn't feel there was much else to be gained by staying around, and if truth was told, he was feeling quite weary. It had been a long, tiring and not exactly uneventful day.

Catching Rawlings's eye, he turned and walked away as the stable team made preparations to unload Choirboy and The Bishop. As Tiny reached his Morgan, Rawlings approached.

"I think I will head for home," Tiny stated decisively, moving towards the driver's door despite not having the keys.

"Right-ho, sir, hop in and we'll be off," Rawlings replied.

Tiny sheepishly moved around to passenger side of the car. He had forgotten that Rawlings had picked him up and had left his own car at Bourne House.

As they slowly made their way back to Oakshaw, Tiny was keen to discover what Rawlings had discovered.

"Apparently all is not well between Chuck and Pam," Rawlings exclaimed authoritatively.

"Oh really?" Tiny replied a little impatiently. "According to whom?"

"Well... one of the stable staff said...."

"Can I stop you right there?" Tiny interjected. "Do you have any actual evidence?" he added rather impatiently.

Rawlings fell silent.

It was starting to get dark as Rawlings parked the Morgan. The day had been long and stressful and Tiny was glad to be home. The two comrades agreed to meet in a couple of days to plan their next move. Rawlings had suggested that he might nose around the yard a little more before they met, to see if there was any further news or update on the investigation. Tiny suspected his interest lay more in the stable staff than the facts, but not having any ideas of his own, he went along with Rawlings's suggestion.

As Tiny headed towards his front door, he said good night to Rawlings and thanked him for driving him.

"I wouldn't have missed it for the world," came the reply. Tiny just smiled and closed the front door.

Chapter Seven

"I have news!" exclaimed a rather excited Rawlings down the telephone.

Albeit a little cynical, Tiny was intrigued by the rather dramatic nature of this statement but try as he may, no further information was forthcoming. Irked a little by Rawlings insistence not to discuss matters over the telephone, they agreed to meet that evening in the Oakshaw Arms. It's all a bit MI5, Tiny thought to himself and doubted very much if the news was exciting enough to warrant anyone listening in on his telephone calls. As he entering the Oakshaw Arms he heard the familiar 'schh....' as a bottle of Guinness (off the warm shelf naturally) was opened and placed on the bar together with a sparkling clean Slim Jim.

"Your usual," Tony stated confidently.

"Thank you Tony, most kind. One for yourself perhaps?" Tiny replied.

"That's much appreciated, just a half of Best perhaps. Nasty business at the racecourse, I hear?"

Tiny had noticed over the years that the best gossips seemed to ask a question with the use of a statement. Tony was a master, although being charitable, and the fact that it was such a major story, perhaps it wasn't surprising that he wanted to talk about it.

Tiny was poised on the cusp of a reply when the door swung open and Rawlings entered. He was relieved; he really didn't know what to say to Tony, and didn't fancy having to explain the day's events to someone who would undoubtedly add a little embellishment of his own before passing it on as fact.

"Can I get you a drink, Mr Rawlings?" Tiny enquired.

"Thank you, sir, a pint of bitter would be much appreciated, and perhaps a packet of crisps?"

Tiny raised his eyebrows but said nothing. This news had better be good, he thought. As they settled in the farthest corner of the bar, he could see that Rawlings was about to burst with excitement.

"Well?" said Tiny with more than a hint of impatience. "What couldn't you tell me over the telephone?"

Rawlings looked left then right before beckoning Tiny towards him. "Cocaine," he whispered. "They found cocaine."

"Cocaine?" Tiny replied, puzzled. "What do you mean they found cocaine? Where? On whom?"

"Choirboy, in the blood sample," Rawlings answered looking a little smug with a 'I told you it was important' look on his face.

Tiny's face widened. Thoughts surged through his brain. He was struggling to make sense of what he was hearing.

"How did cocaine get into Choirboy's system? No wonder he was a little agitated" Tiny stated, thinking out loud.

Rawlings sipped his pint quietly and munched his crisps, saying nothing. He had dropped the bombshell and was now basking in the warmth of the afterglow.

Tiny turned back to Rawlings. "How did you find out?" he asked.

"Well, that's the interesting part..." Rawlings leant forward and continued to pass on the full story making it far more 'cloak and dagger' than Tiny suspected was really the case.

Rawlings had been at the stables when Inspector Stock (accompanied by Sergeant Niven) were leaving the main house. Chuck had marched towards the stables looking concerned and demanding to know the whereabouts of Ian Parkinson. Rawlings had previously seen Ian on the far side of the stable, and deciding to play the innocent bystander, discreetly positioning himself nearby so he could overhear most of the conversation.

There were sixteen stables on the estate housed in two separate buildings. The brick and flint exterior walls were topped with natural slate and featured rather wonky black cast iron guttering that had definitely seen better days. Inside, each building featured eight cubicles with a long corridor running along one side. The exterior wall along the front featured a double wooden door in the centre which allowed access to the corridor and the cubicles inside. Like the rest of the estate, the doors were painted grass green which over the years, and several coats later, had acquired a thick, near varnish type lustre. Inside, each cubicle was fitted out with plywood walls and straw for bedding. The wooden walls were around eight feet high above which, metal rails stretched to the shallow pitched roof above.

As Rawlings stood quiet in a neighbouring stall, Ian was chatting to one of the lads when he heard Chuck, the inspector and Sergeant Niven enter. After sending the lad away on some pointless errand, and after somewhat brief, and pointless niceties, the atmosphere changed and the two policemen commenced a more formal line of questioning. As Ian's answers started to turn increasingly defensive, Inspector Stock suggested they continued the discussion at the police station. Despite raised voices and an extended protest from Ian, Sergeant Niven 'assisted' Ian into the car and they drove away.

"Well, what do you think of that?" Rawlings exclaimed glibly as the story came to an end.

"Think of what? Did you really think Ian wouldn't be questioned?" Tiny asked impatiently. "He is the trainer after all."

Rawlings looked deflated.

"What interests me is the evidence." Tiny continued intently. Rawlings recognised the look on Tiny's face; it was the one he always adopted when a puzzle presented itself, entered his head and refused to leave.

"We need to go to the Estate," Tiny declared. "and first thing tomorrow. There's no time to lose. We need to find out where the cocaine came from, and how it ended up in Choirboy's blood."

"The Estate?" Rawlings enquired. "Do you think the cocaine came from the Estate?"

"Remember Stephen?" Tiny responded. "Do you think that horse's behaviour was so different?"

"Oh… my goodness." Rawlings's face dropped; he hadn't made the connection.

Tiny sat back in his chair with a thoughtful yet satisfied look. The connection with Stephen's death indicated that perhaps this wasn't an isolated incident after all. He gave little thought to the potential dangers that lay ahead. Instead, he concentrated on the puzzle, a puzzle he had to solve, however long it took.

As dawn broke over Oakshaw, Tiny glanced out over what was becoming a familiar morning scene. The regularity of life in the village was fast becoming a comfort to Tiny, a sort of rhythmic certainty that added a degree of reassurance in an ever-changing world.

Tiny didn't have time to dwell. He had agreed to meet up with Rawlings on the Estate at 10.00 am. Although he was determined not to interfere with the police investigation, he also knew the chances of increasing his popularity with either the estate staff or the police was slim. Dressing a little smarter than usual, he refused to admit to himself that secretly he had hopes of 'coincidentally' bumping into Pam.

With breakfast complete, he locked the front door and walked briskly towards his Morgan. This was definitely a day for the roof down, he thought with child-like excitement. Finally, the promise of summer was becoming a reality. It was early May and the sun was shining without a cloud to mask its brilliance. Tiny breathed in the fresh air and looked around at the marvel of nature; it really was a glorious day. Above, a fresh new green was beginning to show on the trees whilst below, the woodland daffodils were quickly being replaced by a carpet of bluebells.

It was 10.00 am on the dot as Tiny parked his car directly outside Rawlings's front gate. Rawlings had heard the unmistakable sound of the Morgan, and greeted Tiny as he climbed out of the car. Rawlings knew Tiny's near obsession with timekeeping and smiled to himself as he recalled one of his familiar sayings: 'No point agreeing a time if you aren't going to stick to it'.

After a brief greeting the two colleagues headed towards the stables. The morning ride out was complete and most of the horses were now back in the yard. Some lads were busy clearing out the stables whilst others were grooming the horses. Rawlings and Tiny decided to split up in order not to appear too obvious, or as Rawlings so delicately put it, intimidating. Whilst Rawlings headed towards to where the grooms were working, Tiny approached Ian, who was talking to Paul Chipping. Ian seemed genuinely pleased to see him, although the same couldn't be said for Paul, who frowned with impatience.

Tiny adopted a casual approach, presenting himself as a concerned friend calling by to check that everyone was okay.

He had no real reason to be on the Estate and he knew his welcome was hanging by a thread. Fortunately for him, neither Paul, Joe nor Ian knew quite what relationship Tiny had with Chuck, so all three were careful not to cause offence.

Unsurprisingly, the presence of cocaine appeared to be a complete mystery to everyone. Paul even had the audacity to questioned the police findings, suggesting that perhaps they had invented the whole story just to discredit the yard though why they would wish to do this he didn't say. Joe tried to be helpful muttering some incoherent rubbish which added nothing to the discussion.

Turning the conversation to more everyday matters, Tiny discovered Choirboy had recently been sent over from Ian's main yard in Galway. Although the Ashbury Estate was his English base it was clear the business was still very much based in Ireland, at least for the time being. As the enterprise expanded, Ian was keen to raise his profile in England and split his operation between Galway and the Ashbury Estate. As he was now training several quality horses for Eben Weller, and considering his association with Chuck, it seemed he had an ideal opportunity to leverage the relationship.

"So, how often do horses travel between the two yards?" Tiny enquired.

"Oh, quite often," Ian replied, "although not always the same ones of course."

Tiny was fascinated to learn how different horses were selected for different events. Some were suited to long races, some to short, some for steeplechase or hurdles and some for flat. Ian talked about the racing season across both countries, and described how horses regularly travelled to and from Ireland competing in the most lucrative events either side of the Irish Sea, or as Tiny rather traditionally knew it, St. Georges Channel.

Paul Chipping looked distinctly sour-faced; it was obvious he disapproved of this amateur with little knowledge of the 'sport of kings' asking damn stupid questions. He made some feeble excuse about needing to be somewhere else and sloped off like a delinquent teenager.

Tiny wasn't too disappointed, since Ian seemed to be far more helpful. "So Ian, this cocaine business, how on earth did it get in Choirboy's blood?" Tiny enquired rather directly.

"Honestly, Tiny, I have no idea," Ian sighed. "The police asked the same question and weren't too impressed that I didn't know the answer."

Tiny hoped Rawlings was having more luck. Apart from learning a considerable amount about racing, he knew little more now than he did when he arrived.

Making his excuses to Ian, Tiny went in search of Rawlings. There were a number of stable staff busing themselves with mucking out and cleaning the tack. A couple were even giving the yard a sweep. Tiny was impressed; his house wasn't as clean as this yard, he thought to himself.

Rawlings was tucked away in the corner of one of the stables, chatting to one of the young stable lads. They appeared to be deep in conversation, so in order not to disturb the flow, Tiny rather unconvincingly pretended to take an interest in his surroundings. Probably a good idea talking to one of the more junior members, he thought. Young people rarely knew how to be discreet, and not being seen as a threat, they often know more about what's going on than their more senior colleagues.

After Tiny had paced around rather awkwardly for a few minutes (subtlety was a skill yet to be mastered), Rawlings arrived by his side.

"Ah...Mr Rawlings." Tiny exclaimed with unconvincing surprise. "Well? What did you find out?" he asked in almost a whisper.

"I spoke with both Gary – that's the young lad over there," Rawlings announced, waving his arms in an indiscreet manner, "and to Samantha." Rawlings added proudly. "Samantha was most helpful..."

"Really?" Tiny snapped. "And what did you find out?"

"Oh...yes...well, they both knew about the cocaine in Choirboy's blood, although they didn't seem to know where it came from. Apparently, a couple of stable staff were caught using illegal drugs while they were working in the Galway yard, but I'm not sure if that's connected. Anyway, Ian dismissed them both apparently. That's about it."

"Interesting..." Tiny replied thoughtfully. "So, Ian knows a little more about drugs than he admitted."

Before either could say any more, they were interrupted by the scrunch of gravel as a familiar blue Ford Sierra pulled into the yard. As Inspector Stock and Sergeant Niven climbed out, neither looked particularly impressed to see Tiny and Rawlings standing between them and the stable staff.

"Good morning Inspector." Tiny said cheerily.

Similar to the stable team, neither the inspector or his sergeant quite knew what relationship Tiny had with Chuck. Inspector Stock was also a little nervous about how many of his senior colleagues Tiny might be acquainted with, and much to Rawlings's amusement, had obviously decided to tread with care.

"Mr Tiny, you again," commented the inspector. "you seem to be here more than we are." He added trying to remain polite yet with a distinct undertone of sarcasm.

"Just checking that everyone is OK after the dreadful events at Newbury," Tiny replied. "I hear cocaine was discovered?"

"And what do you know about cocaine?" came the reply.

"Well, I was just wondering where it came from? Is cocaine a problem in the racing world?" Tiny asked trying to be non-specific.

"Drugs in general are becoming an increasing problem," chipped in Sergeant Niven, "but this is the first occurrence we've had in this area."

Inspector Stock scowled at his sergeant for daring to give away even the most innocent piece of information.

"So, you have no idea how cocaine came to be in Choirboy's blood," Tiny asked directly.

"Not at this stage," the Inspector responded impatiently, "although we're fairly confident it was an attempt to fix the race; nobbling racehorses is not uncommon." He added with a sense of authority.

Tiny made no reply.

In an ill-judged attempt to cross examine, Rawlings jumped in with both feet. "So, your theory is…"

Before Rawlings could finish his sentence, or more importantly, rile the inspector with a completely pointless statement, Tiny intervened.

"Thank you, Inspector, that's an interesting theory. We will let you get on with your enquiries." He added trying hard to close down the conversation.

Rawlings looked irked but decided not to pursue it.

Bidding the inspector and sergeant a good day, Tiny set off back to his Morgan with Rawlings a few paces behind. As Rawlings caught up, his irritation was apparent.

"You didn't believe that nonsense about race fixing, did you, sir?" he asked.

"I'm sure it goes on," Tiny replied without breaking step. "Although with so many legitimate drugs available, I doubt if anyone would use cocaine."

Rawlings's thoughtful look, soon turned to humility as his sense of annoyance melted away. Obvious really; why didn't I think of that? he thought.

"I'm far more interested in what the stable staff told you," Tiny continued. Rawlings detected the underlying complement and was grateful for the gesture.

As they approached the Morgan, the two colleagues both agreed that the key to the case was the discovery of cocaine. Although Tiny accepted the existence of illegal drugs in major cities, for some inexplicable reason, he didn't expect to stumble across them in the idyllic setting of Oakshaw or the Ashbury Estate. During his career, he had become exposed to an increasing number of cases involving drugs, but he knew he was naïve, and smiled to himself when he realised that in his world, he rarely came across anything stronger than aspirin. Maybe judges really are out of touch he thought with a chuckle.

"So, what do we do now?" Rawlings enquired, looking for inspiration. "We are hardly experts in the cocaine trade." He sighed.

"No, we're not... but we know plenty of people who are."

"Do we?" Rawlings replied with a sense of puzzlement.

"We have quite a network, an 'inner circle', you could say," Tiny pointed out.

A vast number of criminals had passed through his court over the years, and he had kept tabs on quite a few. No matter what the crime, or how violent, corrupt, depraved or sinister the subject was, Tiny had seen it all. In his private world, crime was an unfamiliar bedfellow, but in his professional life.... well, maybe he wasn't quite as naïve as people believed.

The penny dropped, and Rawlings became excited. "That's a thought," he said. "Do you have anyone in mind?"

"Umm... Maybe," Tiny replied thoughtfully. "We need to visit London."

"We?"

"Of course," Tiny smiled. "We're a team, and besides, I was hoping you would drive."

Chapter Eight

The train would have probably been easier, but Tiny didn't relish the prospect of public transport, especially to the East End of London. Although he didn't have an exact address, he remembered the general area where the person he had in mind operated, or used to operate before Tiny sentenced him to seven years in prison. Harry Metcalf was what some would describe as a likeable rogue. Tiny preferred the term criminal, although rather strangely he did have an odd sort of respect for Harry. Yes, he was a drug dealer and a successful one at that, however he never engaged in violence, preferring to concentrate on the more peaceful (and lucrative) 'City' market and the growing number of yuppies who followed Gordon Gekko's 'greed is good' philosophy of work hard; play hard. Tiny knew crime was still crime and should not to be condoned however he secretly admired an entrepreneur who spotted a gap in the market and worked hard to fill it. Harry Metcalf was just that sort of person, and would have been a success whichever side of the law he chose to exploit. It was a shame he opted for the 'dark side', to coin another cinematic phrase.

Tiny was looking forward to visiting London, though he couldn't think why. He had been glad to leave, and had settled well into his new country life but still, for some inexplicable reason, he felt quite excited to be returning to 'the smoke', even if it was just for the day.

As the journey progressed Tiny described Harry Metcalf to Rawlings and explained the salient (and publicly available) details of his case. Harry would have probably been released a couple of years ago, and knowing Harry, Tiny thought to himself, he was probably back to his old tricks. The reality of the situation suddenly occurred to Tiny, maybe his welcome wouldn't be quite as warm as he was hoping. Maybe there was more risk than he thought, and with hindsight, perhaps it wasn't such a good idea after all. He decided not to share his growing worries with Rawlings, but it was a comfort to know that he wasn't travelling alone.

Tiny recalled that Harry operated from a base in Limehouse on the north bank of the Thames, just a short, but comfortable distance from his 'City' market. Whilst Limehouse was once in the centre of a thriving dock community, like other areas along the eastern edge of the London, it had recently fallen on hard times and was not a place attractive to outsiders. Most goods now arrived by container, and as the ships grew bigger, poor old Father Thames just couldn't compete with the deeper waters of the coast. Plans were already in place to convert Canary Wharf into a business area, although it was quite a distance from the City and the enormity of the task was putting the project in jeopardy.

Limehouse was an interesting area. It consisted of a blend of residential and commercial property, with a growing number of leisure craft occupying an old dock area known as the Limehouse Basin. Work was also underway on the old railway track along its northern edge with plans to open a new automated light railway service linking Bank Station with the proposed new business district of Canary Wharf. Tiny marvelled at the technology, but felt the world was fast moving out of his reach.

As Rawlings weaved through the London suburbs, Tiny was increasingly grateful that he didn't have to drive. Although he loved his Morgan, it wasn't a car that was happy in congestion. Rawlings on the other hand seemed in his element, reliving the years he had spent driving Tiny across London.

As they entered Limehouse, Rawlings asked the question that Tiny had dreaded.

"We're here, sir. Where did you arrange to meet Mr Metcalf?"

"Ah… well, I didn't exactly arrange to meet him," Tiny replied a little sheepishly, "but this is where he used to operate. I'm sure will can soon track him down." He added confidently.

Rawlings stared at Tiny, but wisely decided to say nothing. An awkward silence continued until Tiny spotted Narrow Street. "Oh yes, this rings a bell." he said. "Can you park here?"

Rawlings pulled into a free space by the side of a street which, when considering the neighbouring vehicles, appeared more used to accommodating old rusty vans and cars that were barely alive. Unfortunately, their presence instantly attracted a number of local youths, who took an unhealthy interest in the Morgan. As Rawlings locked the car and they started to walk away along Narrow Street, Tiny asked rather flippantly, trying hard to lighten the mood "Do you think we'll ever see the car again?"

"Maybe," Rawlings replied, "but I doubt it will have any wheels." Hardly the comforting answer Tiny was hoping for.

Despite living in Mayfair and working in central London for most of his adult life, Tiny felt out of place. Limehouse was about as far removed from his world as it was possible to be, and he knew it. He was grateful now, more than ever that Rawlings was with him. Although his initial thought had been how much easier it would be not to have to drive himself, this was now replaced with how much safer he felt with the presence of his old comrade.

Seeing a newsagent, Tiny thought it would be an idea to make enquiries about the whereabouts of Harry. "I expect they will deliver his newspapers," Tiny said optimistically. Rawlings just smiled; this was a world with which he was far more familiar, and he was bemused by Tiny's naivety. Rawlings was on his 'manor', or one just like it, and could sense just how out of place Tiny felt.

The newsagent dismissed Tiny's attempts to describe Harry and denied any knowledge of him. A little further along, a garage, complete with a petrol pump and overall wearing attendant, gave much the same story. Rawlings spotted a gang of youths on BMX bikes and thought they might know something but as he approached, they scattered.

Seeing a café located some distance further along, the two comrades decided it was time for a little refreshment. The familiar ting of the overhead bell was strangely welcoming as

Tiny and Rawlings entered the deceptively small space. A large glass window to the left gave way to a glazed door on the right hand side. Across the doorway, 'Maggie's café' was coach-painted in burgundy letters. Inside, Tiny looked around at the Formica-topped tables and plastic chairs which when full, accommodated no more than about twenty customers. The counter was at the rear behind which, steam and the smell of chips was evident. The café was about half full, mostly with workmen finishing their lunch. As Tiny and Rawlings were settling into seats by the window, a woman in her mid-fifties wearing a purple nylon tabard approached.

Rawlings took the initiative. "Ham, egg and chips please, and a mug of Rosie for me." (As Rawlings insisted upon calling it).

Tiny never did understand Cockney slang, but not relishing the prospect of deciphering the menu, he decided to order the same. "Earl Grey, perhaps?" he called as the lady was walking back to the counter. Her lack of response made him think maybe she didn't hear; Rawlings however had a different theory.

The café was beginning to quieten down a little when their order arrived. As Rawlings tucked in his meal with gusto, Tiny did his best to appear enthusiastic. To be fair, the tea was fairly palatable although the thick, plain white mugs that would probably bounce if dropped, weren't quite what he was used to.

After his unsuccessful enquiries at the newsagent and the garage, Tiny decided it was Rawlings's turn to ask the questions. After praising the food and service, Rawlings engaged the woman, who turned out to be Maggie, the café owner, in conversation about how the area had changed since he was last in town. Tiny was impressed with this subtler approach, and felt a little embarrassed by his clumsier attempt with the newsagent and garage owner earlier that morning.

Subtle it may have been but the result was the same: No knowledge of Harry Metcalf and no idea where he could be located. Helpfully, Maggie did suggest asking at The Grapes, a public house overlooking the river in Narrow Street. The problem was, it was only half past three, and the pub was now closed until six o'clock.

Tiny suggested they continue to walk west to an area known as Wapping. Tiny had never visited this part of London before but was aware of the dispute some Fleet Street newspaper owners were having with the unions regarding a proposed move. As trade for the many warehouses along the edge of the river was declining, new industry was taking over although not everyone was supportive. After viewing the exterior of the new offices, printworks and associated buildings of News International, Tiny could appreciate the argument. It was hardly central London, he thought to himself, and it would be a shame to see the iconic Fleet Street diminish.

As they turned to head back, the time was already five thirty. It was quite a stride along the Thames path to Limehouse, but eventually, after travelling some distance, they reached Narrow Street. The Grapes was located at the far end, coincidently not far from where Rawlings had parked the car.

It was six fifteen when they entered The Grapes, and both were ready for a drink and perhaps more importantly, a sit down. Established in 1583, The Grapes was one of London's most traditional alehouses, as Tiny and Rawlings discovered from the landlord who was a little disappointed when Tiny ordered a Campari and soda for himself and an orange juice for Rawlings. Although there was plenty of chat, disappointingly, there was no knowledge of Harry Metcalf.

It was still early and the pub was fairly quiet. Tiny and Rawlings took a seat away from the bar in the far corner overlooking the river. "Well, that's disappointing," Tiny sighed, "I really didn't think it would be this difficult to locate him."

"Maybe he's moved away?" Rawlings responded. "You know, a clean start when he came out of gaol" he added.

"Um… maybe. Either way, it seems like we have had a wasted trip," Tiny replied.

The two comrades stared at the river. "I really could do with a beer…" Rawlings began.

Before he could finish the sentence, Tiny interjected, "You're driving, Mr Rawlings, that wouldn't be appropriate"

They continued to stare at the river in silence until both of their glasses were empty. "Well, Mr Rawlings, I think we should head for home before it gets too late," Tiny said decisively.

Neither Tiny or Rawlings had noticed how busy the pub had become; even standing room was now at a premium. With a little bit of a 'push and shove', they slowly started to make their way through the crowd, apologising to each drinker whose arm they nudged. The bar area itself was particularly busy as local workers enjoyed a swift pint before heading for home. As Tiny approached the door, a man, as broad as he was tall, whispered in his ear.

"Leaving already, your honour?"

"Who are you?" Tiny responded with more than a little shock and trepidation.

"You've been making quite a nuisance of yourself asking lots of questions," the man replied. "We've been watching you."

"We...?" Tiny enquired catching sight of a similar sized gentlemen to his left.

With that, Tiny was guided back to a table in the corner not far from where he and Rawlings had previously been sat.

Rawlings seemed bemused, he had no idea that a conversation had taken place and was still set on leaving. Seeing Tiny flanked by two burly men guiding him into the far corner of the bar, he panicked and lurched forward in an attempt to rescue him from a situation he still couldn't comprehend. A third man stepped in and restrained Rawlings, boxing him into an alcove near the bar before 'suggesting' that he behaved.

Unable to assist his comrade, Rawlings remained still as he watched the two men escort Tiny to a small table where a smartly dressed gentleman sat waiting.

As Tiny sat, his two escorts stood back a little to ensure no one came close enough to overhear their conversation.

"Well, I never thought I would see you again, especially in this neck of the woods," the smartly dressed man stated rather impatiently.

"Mr Metcalf?" Tiny enquired, with a growing sense of confidence.

"Yes, I'm Harry Metcalf, and you are his honour Judge Tiny....." A short pause was followed by, "...and you shouldn't be here. You have been asking a lot of questions about me, in fact you're been raising my profile all over the manor which hasn't exactly been appreciated."

"Oh... I'm sorry about that," Tiny responded a little sheepishly. "I was trying to be subtle."

"Subtle?" Metcalf jibed. "You're about as subtle as a train crash." He added irritably, "Why are you here?"

Tiny started to explain that he had retired and had moved away from London. He told Metcalf about the Ashbury Estate, and the incident at Newbury racecourse. Metcalf failed to see how any of this could be relevant to him until the word cocaine popped into the conversation. Metcalf suddenly took an interest.

"What exactly do you want from me?" Metcalf responded, still impatient.

"I reckon, if anyone knows about cocaine, who has it, who supplies it and where it would come from, it would probably be you," Tiny pointed out brazenly. Silence fell. Metcalf just stared.

Tiny suddenly felt nervous. Had he overstepped the mark?

Leaning forward, Metcalf hissed through gritted teeth, "You sentenced me to seven years!"

"I'm well aware of that, Mr Metcalf," Tiny responded with a little more confidence. "You were lucky you didn't get a twelve stretch."

Metcalf was taken aback.

Tiny continued, "I expect your brief warned you at the time that ten to twelve was a likely outcome, and after the trial, probably advised you how fortunate you were only receiving seven?"

"You call seven years lucky! I was innocent!" Metcalf responded defensively.

"Oh come on, we both know that wasn't the case." Tiny was becoming slightly irritated. "Do you want to know why I didn't sentence you to twelve years?" Tiny didn't wait for an answer. to what was obviously a rhetorical question.

"Despite all the crimes you committed, not once did you use violence, not once."

Metcalf looked shocked.

"I appreciate that you were just satisfying a demand from your City clients. Of course, it was illegal, but you seem to conduct your business in a professional manner without using intimidation, violence or threatening behaviour." Tiny added trying to appeal to Metcalf's ego, and judging by the look on his face, it was beginning to work. "I'm here because I need your help," he concluded.

"And why do you think I would want to help you?" Metcalf scoffed.

"Because I was fair, and saw beyond the obvious. For that at least you should be grateful." Tiny returned Metcalf's stare, and continued, "I don't know what you are up to now, and I don't really care. But I need information and I think you can help me."

"Information?" Metcalf enquired. "What information?" He added with a degree of innocence that Tiny considered mildly insulting.

"I doubt if there's much going on in the illegal drug trade that you aren't aware of," Tiny went on with a frown.

"I'm not in that line of business anymore," Metcalf protested.

"Maybe you are, maybe you're not; that's not my concern." Tiny stated raising his hands in a non-confrontational manner. "But if you were, I wouldn't imagine new competition would be welcome?" he suggested mischievously.

"As I say, I'm not in that line of business anymore," Metcalf snapped. After a short pause he added in a more conciliatory tone, "but I might know a couple people that know something."

"That would be greatly appreciated," Tiny replied with relief. He scribbled his telephone number on a beer mat lying on the table in front of him and handed it to Metcalf.

As Metcalf rose from the table, his two assistants moved forward only to be stopped by a wave of the hand from Metcalf.

"I'll be in touch." Metcalf announced concluding to conversation. "And Judge... call me Harry." He added with a wry smile.

"Thank you, Harry, I'm grateful," Tiny replied humbly.

As Harry turned towards the exit, one of his two assistants leant across to Tiny. "Don't worry about your car," he said, "we've been keeping an eye on it. No one would dare mess with Harry." He added with a grin.

Tiny was relieved to hear that his beloved Morgan was OK but the double meaning of the man's words hadn't fallen on stony soil. More than ever, Tiny appreciated that Harry Metcalf wasn't a man to upset.

As Tiny was gathering his thoughts, Rawlings rushed over. "Are you okay, sir?" he asked.

"Yes, yes, everything's fine, don't fuss," Tiny replied, slightly embarrassed. "Mission accomplished, and now it's time to go home."

"You mean that was..."

Before Rawlings had time to finish his sentence, Tiny interrupted. "It was indeed."

Nothing more was said until the two colleagues were out of the pub and walking east along Narrow Street towards the car.

"I hope the Morgan is okay," Rawlings stated rather obviously.

"I don't think we need to worry about that," Tiny replied with a rather smug degree of assurance.

Chapter Nine

It was an uncharacteristically a wet and gloomy day, especially for early June. Tiny had agreed to meet Rawlings on the Ashbury Estate to try and find out the latest news on the police investigation. It had been several weeks since his meeting with Harry but still he had heard nothing. Tiny was convinced Harry would contact him, but logic was beginning to tell him otherwise.

It was near 11.00 am as Tiny turned off the main road and along the narrow lane leading to the Ashbury Estate. The tarmac was covered in mud again, this time from a large vehicle having recently cut away most of the bank on the left-hand side. This irritated Tiny disproportionately as he slithered his cherished Morgan along the lane and into the tradesmen's entrance of the Estate. The rain was starting to ease and had almost stopped as he climbed from the car and made his way to Rawlings's cottage. He remembered the old saying, *'rain before seven, fine before eleven'* which still seemed to be true.

As Tiny knocked on the door it opened almost immediately. Rawlings stood there, already wearing his raincoat and wellington boots. He quickly explained that two horseboxes from the stables in Galway had arrived earlier that morning and were still on site. As he locked the door and hurried down the path, his collar turned up against the final few drops of rain, Tiny remarked, "I think it's stopped." but received no response.

Rawlings seemed keen to get to the stables as soon as possible and Tiny struggled to keep up. He smiled quietly to himself as he thought how dedicated to this mystery Rawlings had become.

As they reached the yard the team from the Galway stables were loading the last horse on to the second horsebox. They looked suspiciously at Rawlings and Tiny but carried on their business without breaking stride. The horses they had previously off-loaded were being given a drink before being allocated stables. The yard was a hive of activity, and Tiny was nervous about getting in the way. Paul Chipping was directing proceedings with Joe Harrison helping the team from Galway. The retained veterinary surgeon, Michael Parker, was also in attendance to ensure all the horses arriving, and leaving, were in good health and had all the relevant paperwork and passports for the journey.

The sun had now broken through and Rawlings looked ridiculous in his monsoon attire. He had spotted Samantha and had already struck up a conversation before Tiny caught up.

"Yes, they come over every couple of weeks during the main part of the season," Samantha commented. Rawlings mumbled some sort of reply which Tiny didn't really hear.

"No, of course not," Samantha responded. "Different horses are trained for different races. Distances, conditions, flat, hurdles or steeplechase, it's all very different." She added with a mild degree of exasperation whilst staring at Rawlings as if he was a complete imbecile. Rawlings looked a little deflated as Samantha caught Tiny's attention, rolled her eyes and walked off.

"Well, that's interesting," Rawlings exclaimed enthusiastically, not in any way deterred.

"It's quite obvious really." Tiny frowned having only learnt the same thing a few weeks earlier but then discretely smiled, as he turned and headed towards the main group.

Over the next half-hour or so, Tiny and Rawlings mingled with the team as they watched the visitors secure the horses they had just loaded, refreshed the feed, then closed the ramp at the rear of the lorry. Once the job was complete, and the obligatory 'goodbyes' undertaken, the lorries pulled away from the stables, keen to make the evening ferry back to Ireland.

As Tiny and Rawlings stood in bewilderment, a familiar dark blue Ford Sierra appeared from the grass verge where it had paused to let the horseboxes leave. Tiny knew an awkward conversation lay ahead, but he needed find out how the investigation was progressing if he was ever to discover who was responsible for the death of Stephen.

Inspector Stock, accompanied by his sergeant, approached Tiny and Rawlings as soon as they left their car.

"Here again, I see!" the Inspector announced with exasperation and more than a little sense of sarcasm.

"Good to see you, Inspector, I'm glad we've bumped into each other," Tiny lied. "I wanted to enquire how the investigation was progressing?"

"I really don't see it's anything to do with you, but if you must know, I think it's all rather straightforward." the inspector stated with a degree of authoritative smugness.

"Straightforward?" Tiny repeated.

"Yes, it's obvious really. We've conducted a full investigation, spoken to all concerned, and in our opinion, it was just a tragic accident."

"That's the royal we, I suppose?" Tiny snapped back sarcastically. "And what about the cocaine?"

"Cocaine?" The Inspector raised his eyebrows. "Well, there was a trace of an illegal substance found in Choirboy's blood admittedly, but we think he must have picked this up from his feed. I expect somebody disposed of something they shouldn't have, and it ended up in the feed by accident."

"So that's it?" Tiny enquired.

"Yes," the inspector agreed. "We've just dropped by to let Mr Stern know that the investigation is over."

"And what about Stephen?" Tiny pressed. "Don't you think the two incidents are linked?"

"Just an accident and completely unrelated. I've told you that before." The inspector replied with even more pomposity.

"And the death of the jockey at Newbury?" Tiny persisted.

"As I have already said, it was just an accident. These things do unfortunately happen; it's a dangerous sport, you know." The inspector was losing patience.

Tiny was growing increasingly exasperated.

Rawlings and Sergeant Niven watched as Tiny and the inspector traded verbal blows in what was becoming a 'tennis' style conversation. It was clear that both were increasingly becoming agitated, with any semblance of reasonable debate long abandoned. Rawlings was starting to become concerned as to where matters might end whilst Sergeant Niven seemed to be enjoying the spectacle.

As matters reached a crescendo, the inspector was the first to break. "Well, that's it I'm afraid," he barked. "That's the end of the matter. I've told you all you need to know and there's" nothing more to be said!"

"The end?" Tiny replied in a rather high-pitched tone. Rawlings knew this was a sure sign that Tiny was beyond irritation and was fast heading into angry territory. "We'll see about that!" He stated boldly as he turned his back on the inspector and started to walk away.

"Now you listen here," the inspector shouted. "This has nothing to do with you. The investigation is over. Leave it to the professionals!"

That was like a red rag to a bull. Tiny spun around and faced the inspector. "Professionals?" he mimicked. "You don't know the meaning of the word. You are a disgrace!"

As he marched back to his car Rawlings scurried behind. It was a few moments before he caught up.

"The man's an idiot!" Tiny exclaimed, just loud enough to ensure the inspector could hear. "An accident indeed, how ridiculous!" he continued as he fumbled with his key before climbing into the Morgan.

"I don't suppose there's much more we can do?" Rawlings whispered, trying hard to calm the situation.

"We'll see about that!" Tiny snapped, slamming the door. He wound down the window and leaned out. "I'll be in touch," he avowed as he started the engine, shifted into first gear and drove away with uncharacteristic haste and impatience.

Tiny didn't enjoy feeling angry. He tried to avoid conflict whenever he could mainly because it ignited a rage inside that scared him a little. Besides, it didn't help his slightly raised blood pressure. It was time to calm down, and to do that he needed to be on his own. Little would be achieved by staying on the Ashbury Estate especially in his present mood. Maybe Rawlings was right and there wasn't anything else that could be done. Was the inspector right too? Tiny mulled the events over in his mind, working out the various scenarios and trying to assess the facts from different points of view. No matter how hard he tried, nothing seemed to make any sense. He needed a break, some down time to put matters into perspective.

Chapter Ten

It was late afternoon a couple of days later when the telephone rang. Tiny didn't receive many calls and was intrigued, especially at that time of the day.

"Good afternoon, sir," came the voice on the other end of the line. "It's Alan Wilson here."

"Alan Wilson?" Tiny enquired before his brain kicked in and quickly added, "Chief Superintendent Wilson?"

"Yes, sir. You have a good memory, but it's Assistant Chief Constable now."

"That's great news, congratulations," Tiny replied. "I didn't realise you had left the Met." He added knowing that he had remained in the Metropolitan Police, he would be addressing himself as Commander.

"Yes, I joined Wiltshire as ACC about three months ago. It's certainly a change from London, but I must say I do enjoy the country life."

"Me too." Tiny replied in a rather unnecessary jolly tone. Suddenly however, the reality of the situation began to dawn on him.

"It's good to hear from you, but I can't imagine this just a social call?" he asked, a little puzzled.

"Well, not exactly, sir." Wilson replied. "I was wondering if I could call in sometime for a chat?"

Tiny didn't give any hint, but he was curious. Had news of his unofficial investigations reached the higher orders? Would he be invited to assist? Suddenly reality hit and his mind flipped to more negative thoughts. As joy turned to concern, he remembered his run-in with Inspector Stock. Perhaps his comments about professionalism had been a step too far. Did he really refer to the inspector as a disgrace? In hindsight, maybe it wasn't the wisest of comments.

Of course, Tiny realised that Wilson's self-invitation wasn't really a request at all. If the ACC of Wiltshire Police wanted a 'chat' he could hardly refuse. Far better to graciously welcome the opportunity; after all, it's better to see the bullet coming, he thought to himself rather dramatically.

After much rustling of diaries, they agreed a date early the following week, (3.00 pm on Tuesday afternoon) and with that, Tiny was once again left alone to ponder his thoughts.

Tiny cast his mind back to dealings he had with Wilson when he was on the bench. He recalled him as being a tough but fair copper, and someone who never presented a case without considerable supporting evidence. Tiny appreciated this careful, methodical approach especially as it made his job, and of course that of the jury, much easier. This was probably one of the main reasons why Wilson conviction rate was so high. Now there's a professional, Tiny thought to himself; no wonder he was promoted.

Understandably, Tiny didn't remember every policeman and official that he encountered during his legal profession, but a few did stand out in his mind. Wilson was one such man, and although he was still slightly worried why the ACC had invited himself for a 'chat', Tiny was actually looking forward to seeing his old acquaintance again.

It was one of those non-descript kind of days that are neither warm or cold, wet or dry, bright or grey. For early June this was quite disappointing, though thankfully the forecast was looking more promising. Tiny had spent the morning in the garden, keeping on top of the weeds and planting out the last of the summer bedding plants. It was Tuesday, and already 2.00 pm when he decided to come back into the house. He needed to change out of his gardening scruffs before meeting ACC Wilson. He had prepared a light afternoon tea of sandwiches and fruit cake for his visitor although admittedly, he did buy the cake from a local bake sale at the village hall. Patricia had been the cook in the family, and the smell of fresh baking as he returned from work was a memory that would live with him forever. On some days the memory of Patricia was becoming difficult to hang on to, but occasionally, and often when least expected, the recollection of her hit him like an oncoming train, overwhelming and all-consuming.

Washed and changed into suitable country attire, and with most of the soil washed from his fingernails, Tiny was ready to greet his visitor. He scurried around the house checking that the cushions were straight, the ornaments were in line and the curtains were pleated just so. Tiny was prepared. He knew it was just an informal meeting, but even so, he wanted everything to be perfect. He paced from the drawing room to the hall, then to the kitchen and back to the drawing room, constantly checking his watch. It was five to three when he noticed a black Ford Granada gently approaching the edge of the green. The highly polished paintwork seemed to emphasise the importance of the man in the rear seat, who appeared to be taking an unusual degree of interest in his surroundings. The uniformed police officer in the driving seat was rather obvious as the car stopped and turned off its engine. After a brief pause, a smartly dressed man in a dark blue lounge suit and shiny shoes climbed from the rear seat.

Alan Wilson was a tall, clean shaven, slim man who Tiny guessed was probably in his mid to late forties, although he would be the first to admit his record of accurately estimating anyone's age was rather poor. Since he had seen him last, it was clear that Alan had aged a little, with a touch of grey now visible around his hairline. Still taking an interest in his environment, Alan gently closed the car door before he turned and headed towards Bourne House. He opened the wrought iron gate and slowly made his way towards the front door. Tiny resisted the temptation to anticipate Alan's arrival; after all, he didn't want to appear too organised. As the bell tinged, he waited a few seconds before opening the door.

"Assistant Chief Constable," he asked as if he didn't know, "How delightful to see you; do come in." Tiny added in a quiet, gentle and rather nonchalant manner. "Would you like some tea? I normally have some at this time of day and was just going to make it."

"Thank you, sir, that would be most welcome," ACC Wilson replied, "and please, do call me Alan."

"Alan," Tiny acknowledged with a slight bow of his head. "Let's move through to the drawing room, and please you must call me Tiny, everyone else does; I left all that formality back in London." He exclaimed rather too enthusiastically.

As Alan settled into one of a pair of wing-backed armchairs on either side of the Adam styled fireplace, Tiny hurried off to the kitchen to 'prepare' the afternoon tea that stood ready. Tiny always found spontaneity worked best if it was planned. He returned in less than five minutes, which gave Alan just enough time to cast his eye around the drawing room and noted two original watercolours by Thomas H. Shepard: one of the Central Criminal Court, Old Bailey, and the other of the Inner Temple. Tiny caught his eye as he entered the room laden with tea, a few sandwich triangles and a couple of slices of fruit cake, all on his best china and neatly laid out on a wooden tray.

"Happy days, don't you think?" commented Alan.

"Ah, well, yes. Interesting times, for sure," Tiny replied diplomatically.

As the conversation inevitably took the long road down memory lane, both Alan and Tiny started to relax and enjoy each other's company. Tiny's apprehensions began to fade as he tucked into a second slice of rich fruit cake. Alan was far less formal that he had expected, though he was under no illusion that the true reason for Alan's visit was yet to become clear. As the conversation veered to and fro, he started to wish Alan would get to the point. He was not a man who entertained procrastination, and was surprised the ACC was not more direct.

Alan welcomed the offer of another cup of tea. The conversation was going better than he had expected although he was still nervous speaking with a man whom he held in such high regard. He recalled the tremendous respect Tiny had earned from the Metropolitan and City Police; even after his retirement, he was remembered as a fair and supportive judge. Mind you, Tiny was known for not suffering fools gladly, and had little patience with arrogance or inefficiency. He generated an air of trepidation especially among some of the younger, less experienced officers, and was unforgiving if he considered their evidence to be poorly prepared. All the same, he was always fair and went to great lengths to consider the human side of everyone involved. Alan hadn't thought their paths would cross again, but here he was enjoying tea with a man who, he considered had an unparalleled level of legal experience.

It was time to get to the point. "Well, sir, I mean Tiny," Alan started nervously.

The atmosphere in the room instantly changed. Tiny knew the main purpose of Alan's visit was about to be revealed, though he still had no idea what it was, or what would be coming next.

"I believe you know Inspector Stock?" Alan continued before pausing for a response.

"Ah, yes, we have met," Tiny replied, trying to hide his slight embarrassment under a neutral tone.

"He mentioned you had taken an interest in the accident at Newbury racecourse," Alan added.

"An accident?" Tiny exclaimed. "Is that what you think it was?"

"That was the conclusion of the investigation," Alan responded, "and as far as I'm aware, they were quite thorough." He added defensively.

"And how about the death of Stephen Cole? Two accidents in a few weeks. Do you not think there's a connection?" Tiny added trying hard to supress his growing irritation.

"Are you linking the two incidents?" Alan asked, leaning forward in his seat.

This was Tiny's chance. If he wanted the police to re-examine this case, this was his one and only opportunity to influence the investigation.

"Cocaine was found in the blood of the horse involved at Newbury, and considering the one that killed Stephen Cole behaved in a very similar way, yes, I would say there's a connection. Of course, there was no evidence of cocaine in the incident that killed Stephen, but I suspect that's only because there wasn't a post mortem on the horse."

Tiny paused mainly to emphasise his point but to also to let Alan absorb what he had just heard.

"Surely you don't believe it's mere coincidence?" he concluding his point. He knew from his previously dealings with Alan that he despised the word 'coincidence', believing it had no place in an investigation.

Alan sat, deep in thought, for what seemed like several minutes. Tiny sipped his tea and polished off the remainder of the fruit cake. He had planted the seed and was quite happy to give it time to grow.

Finally Alan spoke. "I see," he muttered thoughtfully.

"What do you see?" Tiny asked provocatively.

Ignoring the question, Alan added "What else have you discovered? And what evidence do you have?"

These were two very large questions, both of which Tiny feared would arise. It was inevitable really. After all, he had built his whole legal career on making decisions based upon the facts laid before him but of course, Tiny didn't really have answer to either question. Rather than making excuses he decided a more confident approach was needed.

"Inspector Stock and his team didn't really seem interested in looking past their initial assessment," he told Alan. "They weren't too keen on anyone else asking questions either."

"We can't have members of the public meddling in an official enquiry," Alan stated protectively.

"But then I suppose you're not really an average member of the public," he quickly added, seeing from Tiny's expression that he was about to ignite an argument. "If you say there's a link, it's certainly worth closer inspection." He concluded diplomatically.

"Thank you," Tiny replied simply; argument averted.

"You know that I have great respect for you, sir," Alan went on. "You have one of the sharpest legal minds I have ever known, and any assistance you could offer my team would be greatly appreciated."

"I would be happy to help," Tiny responded humbly, with a smile. Alan stood up to leave; it seemed their business was concluded. They shook hands, and Tiny ushered his guest towards the front door. Alan paused in the hallway, as he stepped over the threshold, he turned to Tiny and asked thoughtfully, "I'm not saying that you are wrong, but do you actually have any evidence?"

"Ah… well…nothing documented." Tiny tried again to fudge the issue. "But I'm confident with Inspector Stock's assistance…" he added enthusiastically.

Alan frowned and interrupting Tiny said, "I'll ask Inspector Stock to get in touch; he's a good man and I'm sure he will appreciate your input."

Appreciate my input? We'll see about that! Tiny thought to himself.

Alan continued, "It was lovely seeing you, sir, and thanks again for the tea."

"Under the circumstances, it should be me thanking you," Tiny responded with a broad smile.

No further words were necessary; Alan knew exactly what Tiny was referring to. He was well aware of Inspector Stock's view of Tiny and his 'interference'. He couldn't admit it to Tiny, but he didn't hold Inspector Stock in high regard and was irritated that the connection to the death of Stephen Cole hadn't been made. Maybe Tiny could be useful after all, he contemplated as he walked back to his waiting car. If nothing else, it would certainly keep the inspector on his toes he thought to himself as a grin crept across his face.

As Tiny cleared away the tea tray, he pondered on his conversation with Alan. Evidence, evidence he thought. That's easier said than done; suspecting is one thing, but it was pointless without actual evidence. But does any actual evidence exist? That was the real question he concluded as he wrestled with the dilemma. If Tiny was going to get Inspector Stock to take him seriously, he had to come up with something a little more tangible than just a theory.

Chapter Eleven

The next morning Tiny awoke with renewed vigour. With his conversation with Alan still circling his mind, he felt his investigation had gained a degree of legitimacy. Maybe now he could make progress and finally get to the bottom of what had been going on at the Ashbury Estate.

He decided another visit was in order, so he telephoned Rawlings and invited himself to tea. He wanted to tell his colleague about his meeting with Alan. Rawlings was occupied during the morning, running a couple of errands for the Estate, so they agreed to meet later that afternoon. Tiny filled his morning pottering around in his garden, then decided to purchase a paper from the newsagent across the green. The paper was an excuse really; his main purpose was to speak with Trevor to find out the latest gossip. This wouldn't be construed as evidence, of course, but it might give him a steer as to where to look.

"Good morning, Trevor, I just popped over for a copy of The Times," Tiny said cheerily.

"Good morning to you, sir," Trevor replied upping the level of cheerfulness. "I would have happily brought it over; you only have to ask."

Tiny was quite taken aback. He was impressed by just how helpful all the residents of Oakshaw seemed, especially

Trevor, who was always positive and a friend to all. Tiny felt quite humbled by Trevor's generous offer.

"That's kind of you, but your time is more precious than mine," he replied modestly, watching Trevor scurry around the shop adding more stock to the shelves and tidying up the magazines. After entering into the normal discussion about local events, especially the upcoming village fete, Tiny eventually managed to steer the topic around to the Ashbury Estate. Despite increasingly indiscreet probing (which even Tiny thought was boarding on the obvious), there seemed to be no gossip regarding the use of drugs. Tiny found this quite puzzling. Cocaine was proved to be involved in one 'accident', and he had his suspicions that it was connected to the other; he was convinced the use of illegal substances was not uncommon amongst the stable staff, and would have expected it to be a topic of conversation in the village. A depressing thought perhaps, but maybe Inspector Stock had a point after all.

With newspaper in hand, Tiny said farewell to Trevor and headed across the green and back to his house. Margaret was due, and as always when she visited, she was keen for an update on the investigation. For once he could honestly report that the police were now examining the incident with an open mind, although no actual progress had been made. He had been trying for weeks to give Margaret encouraging news, but his attempts to put a positive spin on little or no information were wearing thin.

With his house now clean and Margaret updated, Tiny's thoughts turned to what actual steps he could take to progress the investigation. After a hearty lunch of sea bream, salad and fresh new potatoes, he was ready once again to visit the Ashbury Estate. He knew that if he became too much of a nuisance, nobody would speak with him. On the other hand, if he didn't ask questions, he would never find out what really happened. He had to strike the balance between nosy and annoying. This was a near impossibility, he chuckled to himself, but at least he now had a little more support and hopefully cooperation from the official police investigation. On the other hand, he also realised his input would be scrutinised at the highest level, though Alan Wilson was inclined to be accommodating, he expected evidence, not conjecture.

It was a busy afternoon on the Estate. As Tiny arrived he spotted Pam Stern and Ian Parkinson observing a couple of yearlings being exercised in the field beyond. Although they were leaning on the wooden post and rail fence with their backs to the drive, it was obvious they were having a fairly intense conversation. After more years on the bench than Tiny cared to remember, he prided himself on his ability to read body language. He liked to think that he instinctively knew if a defendant was lying and was normally good at reading a jury, well most of the time! Drawing upon all his skill and experience, the body language that Tiny was now reading disturbed him. There was obviously more to the relationship between Pam and Ian than he first thought.

After parking his Morgan and meeting with Rawlings, Tiny walked the short distance to the yard and main stables. Rawlings had agreed to chat again to the more junior members of the stable team, while Tiny headed towards Paul

Chipping and Joe Harrison who were re-stabling one of the recently exercised horses. Michael Parker, the veterinary surgeon, stood to one side watching the proceedings.

"Good morning, Paul, Joe. I can see you are both busy so don't want to disturb you," Tiny said cheerfully.

"Oh, it's you," Paul muttered under his breath while Joe just glared gormlessly. "Can we help you?" Paul uttered a little louder. Michael Parker continued to observe but said nothing.

"I'm assisting the police with their investigation." Tiny inaccurately stated, with an uncharacteristic degree of arrogance.

"I thought their investigation was over?" Paul replied with a sense of concern. Joe's interest intensified as he suddenly began to pay more attention to the ensuing conversation.

"Well, just a few loose ends." Tiny replied casually. "I was wondering if you had any idea how cocaine came to be in Choirboy's blood?"

"None whatsoever," Paul declared. "I've already told the police all I know."

"As the behaviour of the horse that killed Stephen Cole appears to be similar, do you think cocaine might have been involved there too?" Tiny enquired provocatively ignoring Paul's last statement.

"Now listen here!" Joe interjected, "That was just an accident!"

"Quite a coincidence, nevertheless, don't you think?" Tiny added turning up the pressure. From the corner of his eye, he noticed that Michael Parker had begun to pay more attention to the conversation although he remained silent.

Paul stepped in before Joe could respond. "I'm sorry, we haven't time to answer silly questions from you. We've told the police all we know, and we're busy, so you will have to excuse us."

With that Paul beckoned to Joe and they both walked away from the yard. Nothing more was said. Once they were out of sight, Michael Parker stepped over to Tiny. "Nasty business," He stated.

"Do you think Choirboy's feed was contaminated with cocaine?" Tiny enquired.

"Not a chance," Michael responded. "A horse wouldn't touch any feed that didn't smell or taste right." He added as he walked away from the yard and towards the on-site office.

Tiny stood fixed to the spot. Rawlings noticed Michael walking away and seeing Tiny stood on his own, sauntered over. "Any luck?" he asked.

"Unfortunately not." Tiny replied in a rather depressed tone. "But Paul and Joe know more than they are telling, I'm sure of that. The vet is no supporter either. How about you?" he asked. "Did you learn anything new?"

"Not really," Rawlings replied, "although you remember I mentioned the incident that Ian dealt with at the Galway yard? Well, apparently the drug involved there was also cocaine."

"Really," Tiny responded with interest, "that must be more than a coincidence, surely the two incidents have to be linked?"

"Oh, and I discovered that Choirboy had only arrived from Ireland the week before the incident at Newbury," Rawlings added.

"Another link!" Tiny replied, growing quite excited. "Now we're starting to make progress." He stated trying hard to convince himself as much as Rawlings.

As the two colleagues discussed the detail, Tiny pondered their next move. Royal Ascot was due to commence in just under three weeks, and again, horses from the Ashbury Estate would be racing. Tiny suggested that they should attend, though considering the latest events he wasn't sure if they would be welcome in the owners' hospitality suite this time. Tiny agreed to arrange for a couple of tickets, although he wasn't looking forward to the exorbitant prices attached to any event with the name 'Royal' in its title.

After walking Rawlings back to his cottage, he said goodbye to his colleague, climbed into his Morgan and started the journey home. He hadn't moved more a hundred yards when he spotted Pam Stern walking alone along the grass verge towards her house. Dressed in a sleeveless floral dress, she looked quite a picture against the perfect backdrop of the English countryside, however as Tiny approached, it became clear that she had been crying. He stopped the car and turned off the engine. Pam seemed embarrassed to be seen in such a state, and it was obvious she didn't really want to talk with anyone, but as Tiny had already stopped, it was too late for either to avoid even the briefest of conversation.

Tiny climbed from the car and greeted Pam with some pathetic comment about the weather. After more years than he cared to remember, he had given up on being good at small talk and now just accepted the awkward nature of his interaction with pretty much everyone. Saying that, it was even worse with a lady in tears, especially an attractive one. "Is everything okay?" he enquired rather pointlessly; clearly it wasn't.

"Oh… hello Tiny," Pam replied trying to sound surprised. "Yes, everything is fine."

"I noticed you earlier, when I arrived. You were speaking with Ian?" Tiny probed undiplomatically. Almost instantly Pam welled up and fought back more tears. Tiny decided to change tact and fast; he never did know what to say when a woman started to cry.

"I haven't seen Chuck lately?" he said lamely.

"No, he's away at the moment on business," Pam replied, trying to recover her composure and dabbing her eyes with a tissue. "Sorry, Tiny, hay fever, you know; it gets me every year." She lied unconvincingly.

"Ian and I were discussing the details for Ascot. It's only a few weeks away and there is still much to do," she added.

"Ah yes, of course." Tiny replied, relieved. The noticeable stress that was previously in the air was starting to diminish. "I was just discussing the very same with Rawlings."

"Are you planning to go?" Pam enquired.

"Well, Rawlings seemed keen so I said I would tag along," Tiny replied nonchalantly, pretending he wasn't bothered.

"Wonderful, it would be good if you could come along with us. I'll fish out a couple of VIP tickets for you both," Pam offered.

"That's very kind, but I don't want to put you to any trouble?" Tiny responded modestly whilst not insisting too much in case Pam changed her mind.

"No trouble at all," Pam replied. "Come up to the house the next time you are on the estate and I'll have them ready for you."

Tiny thanked Pam for her generosity and assured her that he would collect the tickets as soon as possible. With their business concluded, Pam seemed anxious to leave, so without pressing matters any further, he wished her good day and climbed back into the Morgan.

During the journey home, Tiny thought again about Pam and how seeing her so upset had affected him. He didn't believe for one minute her claim of hay fever, though he had no idea what had distressed her. It was obviously something to do with her conversation with Ian, but what? Tiny had always found Ian to be a most reasonable and likeable chap, and couldn't really imagine he would make a lady cry, well not on purpose. Of course, he didn't know Ian's personal arrangements but whatever they were discussing, it had definitely upset Pam.

As Tiny made his way back home he recalled his earlier conversation with Joe and Paul. Time in the Morgan was always enjoyable and now, having had a little time to relax, he was disturbed by how matters were left. It's not constructive to be so challenging, he told himself; far better to be their friend, gain their trust and appear to be on their side. He should take a lesson or two from Mark Antony's famous Shakespearian speech he huffed. As Tiny mulled matters over in his mind he began to feel depressed; he had never been 'one of the boys', and didn't find it easy. Anyway, whether his approach was right or wrong, he certainly wasn't making the progress he had hoped. He didn't feel he knew any more now than when he started.

After about twenty minutes of tranquil driving through some of the most beautiful countryside in England, Tiny arrived back in Oakshaw. It was a delightfully warm early summer evening; the air was still, with just a hint of twilight tinting the horizon. The days were really stretching out now with memories of long winter nights all but gone. Tiny felt at peace, albeit still a little depressed, as he parked the Morgan, pulled the roof up and walked across to the house. Any arrogance he had felt earlier had long gone and now, he just wanted to listen to the evening concert on Radio Three, or the Third Programme as he used to know it, pour himself a sizeable malt scotch, and relax in his chair. On such a beautiful evening, the thought of going over to the pub had lingered momentarily in his mind, but he decided he couldn't face company, and preferred to be alone with his thoughts.

Tiny had just settled in for the evening. He had exchanged his shoes for slippers and with the Third established on the wireless, he was disturbed by a rather firm knock at the door.

He really didn't want to speak with anyone, and with visitors to his house a rarity, especially at this time of the evening, Tiny was a little irked as he rose from his armchair and walked into the hall. He pulled open the heavy front door and was quite taken aback. Before he could utter a word, the caller lifted his hat and politely, and rather humbly said,

"Good evening, sir. I hope you don't mind me calling at this late hour."

"Inspector Stock, this is a surprise; how nice to see you." Tiny replied almost instinctively. At least the first half of his greeting was sincere he thought, reserving judgement on the second.

"ACC Wilson suggested I called." The inspector added in a tone akin to a school boy apologising to the headmaster.

Tiny made an effort to extend the olive branch. "Ah, yes... Do come in. I've just poured myself a scotch; would you like one?"

"I shouldn't really, sir, I haven't quite finished my shift."

"I won't tell if you don't."

"Well, maybe just a small one, thank you, sir."

"Oh, just call me Tiny, everyone else does. I left all that formality behind when I moved out of London." Tiny exclaimed with ease; he was getting well versed in using that phrase.

"Thank you, sir... I mean Tiny and my name is Matt, after all, I doubt if you want to keep calling me Inspector!"

Tiny wasn't really bothered either way but took the gesture as it was intended.

"Well then; Matthew it is." Tiny proudly announced. He never shortened anyone's name on principle even if they preferred it. 'That was the name they were christened with and that's the name they should use,' he used to say to anyone who asked, which of course was normally very few, if any.

The two men settled in the drawing room, and Tiny handed Matthew a modest scotch; it was a particularly fine Oban 14 and he was reluctant to be over-generous. Tiny decided to let the inspector start the conversation; it was he who had called to speak to him after all. The inspector, stammering nervously, mentioned that ACC Wilson had reviewed the case and had suggested that he engaged with Tiny to ensure local knowledge was taken into consideration. Tiny responded with a little background to his relationship with Alan, and to establish his credentials, he briefly summarised some of the more memorable cases Alan had brought before him. If Tiny was to build any sort of relationship with Matthew Stock, he knew he had to ensure that his point of view would be respected and listened to. Tiny finally brought the conversation around to the incident at Newbury and the death of Stephen Cole. He described why he thought there was a connection during which the inspector listened intently without uttering a word. To add a little weight to his point, Tiny mentioned the reports of cocaine use at the Galway yard, but since that was merely hearsay, he was careful not to overplay his hand. Finally, the inspector spoke.

"That may well be the case, but I still think it was an accident. Choirboy picked up traces of cocaine from his feed and possibly the horse that killed Stephen did the same."

"Not according to the vet." Tiny announced in a soft yet firm tone. "He assured me that there is no way any horse would eat contaminated feed."

The inspector was taken aback. "You've spoken to the vet?"

"Of course. Haven't you?"

Silence ensued.

Chapter Twelve

Tiny had collected his Ascot Royal Enclosure tickets for himself and his 'plus one' from Pam a week earlier. This level of entry was reserved exclusively for invited members and their guests, and Tiny felt suitably privileged to be included. Pam had seemed quiet and a little distant when Tiny had called around, and although he had hoped that he would have been invited in for a cup of tea, no such offer was made. He wanted to delve a little deeper into the conversation he had observed between her and Ian but it was clear she didn't want to talk. Chuck had recently returned from his business trip, and from what Rawlings had reported, the atmosphere around the Estate was noticeably tense.

Tiny was quite excited about visiting Royal Ascot, especially as his tickets were for Thursday 20th June, otherwise known as 'Ladies' Day. He didn't really understand why he found the prospect so appealing especially after the tragic events at Newbury. Maybe it was because it had the word Royal in the title, and the Queen and probably other Royals were due to attend.

In his naivety, Tiny hadn't realised that men entering the Royal Enclosure were required to wear formal morning dress including a waistcoat and top hat. As a result, he had endured quite a busy week, as a quick rail journey to London was required to hire the necessary regalia which was now successfully laid out in the spare bedroom awaiting the time to serve its duty.

Although Tiny had previously promised Rawlings that he would get tickets so they could go together, that was before Pam kindly offered Royal enclosure VIP entry. It was quite a treat to be invited to such a prestigious occasion, and Tiny thought carefully how Rawlings would fit into such surroundings. He didn't want him to feel awkward or embarrass anyone and of course, he would need to hire a suit which was neither cheap, or available locally. Saying that, a promise is a promise and thinking about the reasons why he was attending and how disappointed Rawlings would undoubtably feel, it was right that they went together. Besides, Rawlings had agreed to drive and in reality, Tiny didn't really have anyone else to ask.

Although Ascot was probably only a forty-minute drive on a normal day, an early start was advisable especially as the traffic promised to be challenging. The programme stated that racing didn't start until early afternoon following the Royal Parade, which apparently was a daily occurrence during the festival. All very exciting, Tiny thought as he planned the day in his head. Rawlings arrived on the doorstep of Bourne House at around 9.30 am. As he opened the door, Tiny was surprised to see Rawlings suitably, and so smartly attired in full morning dress.

"Good morning, Mr Rawlings. You look very smart. It fits well for a hired suit."

"Hired?" Rawlings replied. "Oh no, this is one of the suits I used to wear in the hotel." He added proudly.

Tiny decided not to enquire to closely whether the hotel knew that their former employee was still making use of company uniform choosing instead just to be grateful to have a driver for the day.

It was nearer 10.00 am when they eventually set off. It was a sultry day, hot and sticky, and Tiny was keen to get the roof down on the Morgan. Whilst quiet country roads were perfect for open top motoring, motorways were less fun with a little too much turbulence for comfort. As the journey to Ascot involved mainly motorways, they sweltered with the roof up, but at least they could talk without having to shout at each other. As the journey progressed, they discussed the day ahead. Rawlings mentioned the excitement around the Ashbury Estate, especially regarding the second race, The Norfolk Stakes, where their own horse Gypsy Whistler was currently favourite to win.

The forecast of traffic was sadly all too accurate, and it was nearly two and a half hours before they finally arrived in their designated car park. Tiny was in awe of the spectacle laid out before him, stretching nearly as far as the eye could see. There were several helicopters parked on the far side of the course, and another came in to land as Tiny and Rawlings climbed out of the car. "Wow, what a place!" Rawlings exclaimed. Tiny remained silent but inwardly echoed Rawlings's sentiment.

As they wandered towards the entry gate, they were surrounded by crowds of racegoers all dressed in their finest attire. Tiny couldn't remember when he had seen so many people dressed so elegantly, and the colours; this was shaping up to be a very special day he thought to himself. Rawlings was also loving the spectacle, and had a slight swagger in his walk as they strolled past the Village Enclosure, then the Windsor, on past the Queen Anne and towards the exclusive, invitation only, Royal Enclosure.

The arrangement was similar to Newbury racecourse but on a much grander scale. Along the edge of the course was a grass area, probably fifty yards wide, leading to a magnificent grandstand three storeys high and crowned with a prominent, four-sided clock tower. Whilst the Village Enclosure was on the far side of the course, all the other enclosures were adjacent to the grandstand. The Windsor Enclosure was furthest away whilst the Queen Anne and Royal Enclosures split the grandstand in two with the parade ring occupying a central location between them.

As Tiny and Rawlings approached the entrance gate, the queues were already starting to gather. As they waited patiently in line, the experience was best described and polite jostling as everyone pushed eagerly for entry. Security guards were processing people as quickly as possible, however the IRA bomb at the Conservative conference in Brighton the previous October had heightened security and matters were taking time. A scuffle, quickly quelled, broke out to Tiny's right between two 'gentlemen' who both thought they should have been next in line. Tiny was happy to wait patiently.

Finally, and after around fifteen minutes both Tiny and Rawlings found themselves inside and in lavish surroundings as they mingled amongst the elite. Whereas the men were all dressed the same, in either black or grey morning suits; the ladies were finally on parade. Some of the dresses were glamorous to the point of being outrageous and though a hat was obligatory, some were barely more than a feather while others were the size of a small planet. Tiny was intrigued by the spectacle, and relished the sheer Britishness of the whole occasion.

Rawlings seemed a little too keen on admiring the ladies' outfits, especially the more extrovert ones. When Tiny suggested they should move towards the owners' area, he reluctantly obliged. As they made their way into the grandstand and up to the top floor, they bumped in to Ian who was heading in the same direction with a group of other trainers. Not realising they weren't permitted into the owners and trainers' area they tagged along only to be denied entry on the door.

"Oh, I'm sorry, old chap," Ian muttered rather unsympathetically as the official refused admission. "I'm afraid this area is restricted."

Tiny was taken aback, not so much by being refused entry but more by Ian's coldness. Without responding or giving any hint of his annoyance, Tiny turned to Rawlings and proposed that they explore the members' bar. Ian had long disappeared with his pals and was no longer in sight. Rawlings, looking a little puzzled, agreed to Tiny's suggestion. As they entered the bar, crowds were starting to fill the room though it was still an hour before the start of the first race.

With so many people, and no one from the Ashbury Estate in sight, Tiny was beginning to wonder why he had come. Though he relished in the splendour of the occasion, his purpose was to find more about the activities of the horses trained by the Ashbury Estate, and the possible use of drugs. So far, apart from obviously alienating Ian, though he didn't know how, he had learnt nothing.

Rawlings had only just left to collect a couple of drinks from the bar, using Tiny's fiver of course, when Tiny spotted Pam and Chuck near the balcony. Making his way through the crowd Chuck caught sight of him approaching and with a smile that would have brightened the dullest of days, he greeted him like a long-lost friend. Conversely, Pam looked sheepish, barely managing a wry smile. As Chuck vigorously shook Tiny's hand to a point of near dislocation, Rawlings approached with the drinks.

"Glad you could make it, old chap!" Chuck boomed. "And your plus one!" he laughed, catching sight of Rawlings.

Rawlings was not amused but said nothing. Tiny was bemused but taking Rawlings lead, also made no reply.

"Isn't this just the best occasion?" Chuck continued with infectious enthusiasm.

"It certainly is," Tiny responded. "I bumped into Ian earlier..." Pam went white wondering what was to follow. "But I haven't seen anyone else from the Estate?" Tiny continued. Pam looked significantly relieved and as colour once again filled her cheeks. "They are all here somewhere," Chuck replied, looking around the room expectantly.

As the conversation continued, Chuck mentioned that Paul, Joe and the team of grooms had all been busy ensuring the star of the afternoon was ready for the second race of the day. As Chuck talked enthusiastically about Gypsy Whistler there was a sudden change in atmosphere, as the crowd began to move across to overlook the parade ring.

"Oh, the Royal Parade must be about to begin," Chuck exclaimed with the delight of a schoolboy. Just then, an announcement came over the Tannoy system announcing exactly that as the remainder of the room hurried to view the spectacle.

As Tiny, Chuck, Pam and Rawlings reached the outside balcony, the royal coaches were making their way around the ring before heading out on to the course. The coaches looked to be grand affairs, lifted straight from a Victorian novel. Open and with seating for four people (two facing front, two aft), they were each drawn by a stunning pair of grey mares. A brightly dressed coachman in a red tunic with gold braid rode one horse while managing the second. A pair of footmen rode at the rear of the coach wearing, what appeared to be a red, single-breasted dinner jacket with white tie and top hat garnished with gold braid.

The first coach which led the parade, was occupied by the Her Majesty, Queen Elizabeth II, who was wearing a yellow-green dress and matching hat. She was accompanied by Prince Philip, the Duke of Edinburgh, dressed in a black morning suit and top hat and seated next to her. Behind the Queen's coach, Princess Diana, the Princess of Wales, wearing a peach-coloured dress and wide brimmed hat, was accompanied by the Queen Mother who wore a turquoise floral outfit. Smiles beamed all around as the royal party proceeded around the ring and then, to mounting cheers, became visible to the crowds along the side of the course.

As soon as the procession was out of sight, most of the crowd surrounding the parade ring and filling the balconies returned to the bar and hospitality areas. Chuck made his excuses, explaining that he needed to check on Gypsy Whistler, and quickly hurried away. Rawlings seemed interested in placing a wager on the first race and had vanished into the crowd, leaving Tiny alone with Pam.

Alone of course is a relative term, as several thousand other people made the prospect of quiet conversation quite impossible. All the same, neither Pam or Tiny paid any attention to the throng around them, who in their excitement, were oblivious to the melancholy of Pam and the awkwardness felt by Tiny.

As Tiny escorted Pam back into the bar, he sensed her unease. As they resumed their previous position in the far corner of the room, he felt he should say something.

"Is everything okay?" he enquired.

"Of course. Why shouldn't it be?" Pam replied rather coldly.

"I'm not here to judge, but you do seem a little on edge?"

"Like you don't already know!"

Tiny looked confused. "I don't know anything," he responded trying hard to adopt a neutral tone.

"Chuck isn't an easy man to live with."

"Ah… I see," Tiny replied, trying hard to sound sympathetic and in so doing, encourage further revelations.

"And he's away quite a lot," Pam went on, stifling a sob. "And I get lonely on my own."

"How long has it been going on?" Tiny asked, gambling that Pam was keen to get whatever it was off her chest.

It was like opening a floodgate. Pam described at length how she and Ian had been involved for over a year, and while she was sure Chuck didn't suspect, Ian was worried that his wife was becoming suspicious and would soon realise something was wrong.

"Chuck's too busy to notice anything about me," Pam added as she started to sob, "but if the market shifts a few points, or one of his companies has a wobble, it's like he has a sixth sense."

Tiny didn't really know what to say. He felt humbled that Pam should confide in him, but a little embarrassed by her frankness. As Pam was being so honest, and thinking that perhaps he wouldn't get a second chance, Tiny decided to see what he could find out about the reports of cocaine on the Estate.

Pam seemed relieved to move the conversation on from her own problems. "Ian knows there are drugs on the Estate, and it's not just cocaine. It's been going on for quite some time," she told him. "Some of the grooms and stable lads sometimes use a little a pick-me-up, as Ian calls it, but things seem to have got out of hand lately."

"Where does it come from?" Tiny asked, trying hard to keeping his questions short and direct so as not to interrupt the flow.

"I have no idea," Pam stated emphatically.

"I hear the Irish yard in Galway may be involved?" Tiny was fishing and suspected Pam knew it.

"Really? If that's the case, goodness knows where they get it from. All I know is that Chuck has been mixing with some very unsavoury characters lately. One minute he says his business isn't doing well, and the next minute...well, he seems to have plenty cash to burn. Take this racing caper, for example. That can't be cheap!"

Tiny was about to ask another question when Rawlings returned, proudly clutching a betting slip for the first race.

"I had a tip!" he exclaimed. "And they'll be off in a couple of minutes." He added excitedly failing to notice that Pam had been crying. As Tiny congratulated his colleague, he ushered him away towards to balcony overlooking the course, ready for the off. Pam melted into the crowd as Tiny and Rawlings readied themselves for the first race of the day. As Rawlings chatted excitedly, Tiny tried hard to respond with the appropriate nod and occasional agreement but his thoughts were elsewhere. His eyes darted across the room trying to spot Pam, but she was nowhere to be seen. As the balcony filled with excited racegoers readying themselves for the first race, Tiny's view became obscured with everyone pushing to look out across the course. Reluctantly, he had little choice but to abandon his thoughts as 'They're off!' echoed around the course.

"But it was such a good tip," Rawlings complained. "I was assured it would win; it was a cert." he continued with a degree of puzzlement.

"I think that's why they call it gambling." Tiny responded rather philosophically. "Besides, he was pretty close and second wasn't a bad result." Tiny added trying hard to lift his colleague's spirits.

Rawlings remained silent as he tore his betting slip in two.

As the horses collected back in the parade ring, now dubbed the winners' enclosure, the crowd shifted and gathered on the balconies on the opposite side, away from the course. As the jockeys dismounted, their grooms were standing by to remove the saddles and quickly replace them with a sponsors' blanket. Stables lads were offering buckets of water to the horses, as the owners and other dignitaries gathered for the presentation. Two or three young men with shoulder-mounted television cameras were moving through the crowd, attached by wires to a presenter who was interviewing anyone who passed by.

As events unfolded, the crowds parted, lining up ceremoniously as one of the more junior royals moved towards the podium to present the winning jockey and owner with a huge, oversized trophy. Once the obligatory handshakes and photographs had been completed, the young royal returned to the Royal Enclosure and the horses we quietly led away.

"Gypsy Whistler is up next," Rawlings stammered eagerly. "Now that has to be worth a punt!"

Tiny smiled; it seemed the disappointment of the first race had now become a distant memory as he agreed that they should support the home team.

Rawlings caught sight of one of the Estate staff and pushed through the crowd, leaving Tiny behind. He was a little irked that Rawlings had disappeared without agreeing to place a wager for him, but then again, Rawlings wasn't really there to attend to his needs Tiny thought to himself.

Being alone, Tiny decided to explore a little and work out for himself how to place a bet. After all, it couldn't be that difficult and besides, he was sure the trackside turf accountants would be more than willing to help him especially as there was a good chance, he would never see his money again.

The group had moved on, and although there were crowds around him, Tiny was on his own. He felt a little awkward standing there in his best finery with no one with him. He was still not used to being without Patricia, and there were times, which admittedly were becoming fewer, when the enormity of the loss struck him. Feeling self-conscious, and strangely sad especially amid such joy, Tiny quietly made his way down the stairs before exiting into the fresh air. Taking a deep breath, he smiled to himself knowing that Patricia would have told him to get a grip and not to be so stupid.

Pushing through the mass of racegoers, he decided to move across to the Queen Anne Enclosure which neighboured the other side of the parade ring. There seemed to be more life on that side of the fence, and Tiny was intrigued to see where regular people spent their day. Of course, there was nothing ordinary about the whole occasion, and upon entering the Queen Anne Enclosure, everything was much the same, albeit the men were wearing lounge suits rather than the more formal morning attire. There did however seem to be more entertainment on offer including a small sectioned-off area on the grass where afternoon tea was being served. There was a Pimms' bar, several champagne bars and an Irish bar serving a range of traditional stouts. In fact, every sort of bar you could imagine, and as long as you had deep pockets, there was no excuse to go thirsty at this event!

Finally, and after considerable effort, Tiny managed to push through the crowd's and reached the area where the trackside bookies were plying their trade. He knew the Tote, (being government owned) was known to be safer, although he had no idea why. He had also heard the minimum stake allowed on the Tote was lower, but it didn't seem as much fun as doing business with a man standing on a crate and surely fun was what the whole day was about.

Looking along the row of tic-tac bookies, the odds seemed to be identical, so choosing one at random, he placed his bet. As he stuffed the ticket into his pocket, he noticed a couple of obvious plain-clothes police officers moving through the crowd. As he moved away from the crush into a little space towards the grandstand, he caught a glimpse of Inspector Stock chatting to a rather irritated bookie. There appeared to be much waving of hands however as Tiny approached, the conversation seemed to be nearing its end as the bookie walked off muttering something about harassment and upsetting his customers.

"Inspector… sorry, Matthew. I'm surprised to see you here?" Tiny said.

A rather startled Inspector turned to greet him. "Oh, hello, sir. I didn't realise you were here today."

"I was invited by the Sterns; they have a runner here, in fact it's the favourite in the next race." Tiny replied whilst being rather impressed by how natural his horse-related phraseology had become.

"I assume by the presence of your colleagues that you are not here for pleasure?" he continued.

"No, indeed not. Following our little chat, I think you may have a point. We are now working on the theory that the death of Stephen Cole and the incident at Newbury are related."

"I see; I was happy to help," Tiny replied. "Tragic events, but I'm pleased you no longer think they we accidental," he added, trying to strike the right balance between humility and concern.

"Your persistence was very much appreciated." The inspector lied with false sincerity. "We have now widened the investigation. I'm not sure if you realise that the problem stretches far beyond the Ashbury Estate."

"You mean the smuggling and use of illegal drugs?" Tiny enquired excitedly.

"Drugs?" The Inspector looked puzzled. "No, that was that was just coincidence, we think there's race fixing going on." He added with a childish sense of pride.

"Race fixing?" Tiny was aghast.

"Yes, we are investigating a gambling syndicate…"

Before the inspector could finish his sentence, his words were drowned out by the public address system announcing the runners were making their way to the start line for the second race, the Norfolk Stakes.

Not wishing to sour his new, more cordial relationship with the inspector, or miss the race, Tiny made his excuses and hurried back to the Royal Enclosure to view the action. On the way he tried to comprehend how the police were so adamantly against anything to do with drugs. Surely, they can't believe it was coincidence but maybe a gambling syndicate? Tiny was beginning to question. Maybe there was more to this than he first thought; maybe the police were one step ahead? Casting his mind back to Inspector Stock, he considered that hypothesis most unlikely.

Tiny reached the Royal Enclosure's hospitality bar just as the horses were heading out onto the course. Chuck, Pam and the team were standing together on the balcony as Tiny made his way across. Champagne was flowing freely however before Tiny could collect a glass, Chuck spotted him approaching. Placing his arm around Tiny's shoulder, he guided him away from the crowd in a swift movement that left no choice other than to comply. Once away from the overhearing ears of the others, a serious look came over Chuck's face.

"Tiny's old chap, can I ask an enormous favour?"

Tiny felt a blend of worry and embarrassment, partly by how close Chuck was to his face but mainly by what was coming next.

"Sure, ask away, although I can't make any promises." He replied nervously.

"Of course, I understand. It's just that...well, I'm becoming a little concerned about what's going on in the stables."

"You mean the drugs?"

"Drugs? Chuck responded, "The police mentioned race fixing?"

"Oh, I see...yes, I hear the police have a theory."

"A theory? You don't believe they have any proof? And what's this about drugs?"

Trying hard not to comment on the allegation of race fixing, Tiny continued. "The police mentioned that cocaine was found in Choirboy's blood and..." Before Tiny could finish his sentence Chuck impatiently interrupted. "Yes, yes, they mentioned that but they didn't seem to think it was relevant, after all, it was only a trace."

"That true but there's also a suggestion that recreational drugs are commonplace in the yard and maybe in the Galway yard too."

"Chuck was silent; either he was blissfully unaware or was worried by the extent of who knew what.

"Commonplace? And in Galway too?" Chuck repeated thinking aloud. After a short pause, he continued. "I need to know what's going on, I don't suppose you could dig around a little for me?"

Tiny didn't reveal that he was already doing just that but he was slightly worried whether Chuck actually wanted to find out the facts or just wanted a man on the inside, to keep him informed on the progress the police were making.

"Well, I suppose I could ask a few questions," Tiny responded in a nonchalant manner, "just to see what I can find out."

"That would be great; thank you so much, I would really appreciate if you could keep me informed."

Tiny's suspicions grew stronger but nevertheless, smiled in agreement. Before either could utter another word, Pam wondered over.

"You two look very serious?" Pam enquired with a worried smile. "Come on, they're almost in the starting gate."

"Just discussing the form my dear; Tiny's really getting into the racing spirit! Didn't I tell you he would!"

Chuck snapped back to his old self just as 'They're under starter's orders' echoed across the course. Chuck moved over to the edge of the balcony holding a pair of binoculars, with Pam standing just behind. As she caught Tiny's eye, she smiled rather sheepishly before swiftly gazing out across the excited crowd and the track beyond. Rawlings was standing

146

on the opposite side next to Joe Harrison, who was chatting to a couple of wealthy looking businessmen. Despite the frivolity of the day, they seemed strangely serious, and out of place at such a joyous event.

The noise level rose a couple of notches as 'They're off!' was drowned out by a cheer from the crowd. Tiny was instantly caught up in the infectious excitement that surrounded him, and remembering the previous events at Newbury, became quite anxious as the horses thundered down the home straight. The volume of the crowd continued to rise as cries of encouragement quashed any chance of conversation. Tiny thought this was quite strange as he was sure the horses, or their jockeys couldn't really hear individual comments, and even if they could, he doubted it would make them try any harder.

As the first of the chasing pack crossed the line Tiny found himself surrounded by disappointment; Gypsy Whistler had been beaten by a nose. Chuck bowed his head and banged his fist on the ledge. Pam took a step back not wishing to obstruct her husband while on the opposite side, Joe Harrison stood motionless with a gormless expression on his face. This struck Tiny as odd; he would have expected more reaction from the assistant trainer. Before he could give it any more thought, Rawlings walked over.

"I can't believe it, so close, I was assured he would win. That's ten pounds down the swanny!" he exclaimed.

"Well, that's why..."

"Yes, I know, that's why it's called gambling." Rawlings mimicked. "I won't be needing this!" he exclaimed tearing up his betting slip and tossing it into a nearby bin. "Did you lose much? I assume you also had some money on Gypsy Whistler?"

"Yes, indeed..."

"You must be disappointed too?

"A little I suppose, but I thought it was safer to opt for a three-way. The odds were only even but still, something is better than nothing. I don't suppose you could pop down and collect my winnings for me, old chap? I wouldn't mind a quick word with Chuck."

Rawlings face needed to be seen to be believed as he quietly took the betting slip from Tiny and headed towards the door.

Tiny moved over to the balcony and placed his hand on Chuck's shoulder.

"Bad luck, old chap. You must be very disappointed."

Chuck looked up solemnly. "I really needed that win." He sighed quietly. Tiny was taken aback; here was a man who was clearly more than just disappointed. An afternoon of fun and excitement had long since evaporated and a more serious atmosphere now hung in the air.

The two businessmen that Joe had been speaking with earlier were glaring at Chuck, who purposely avoided their stare. As they turned and walked briskly away, Tiny was struck by how affected Chuck was. Surely a win couldn't be that important? Conversely, Joe just remained still not really knowing what to do with himself. He looked awkward, nervous and somewhat out of place. Making some feeble excuse, he was just leaving as Pam and Ian appeared. Forming a huddle with Chuck, they were deep in conversation when Rawlings arrived back. Handing over Tiny's winnings, it was clear the fun of the day had disappeared for him too. Looking over at Chuck, Pam and Ian who were still whispering feverishly, it was apparent to Tiny that he and Rawlings were very much the outsiders. Making their excuses, they made their way down the stairs and outside towards the parade ring.

Tiny spotted a tranquil corner where afternoon tea was being served, and suggested they pause for a while to discuss the events of the day. Although by now the third race was already over, there was still the Gold Cup ahead and the fifth and sixth races but Rawlings, having lost his appetite for gambling, eagerly agreed. As the Earl Grey and three-tiered plate of sandwich fingers and assorted fancies arrived, they took stock of the day.

"It's a shame about Gypsy Whistler." Rawlings commented. "It was so close."

"Chuck seemed inconsolable," Tiny replied. "And who were those two businessmen speaking with Joe?"

"I'm not sure; I think they were Irish, and they definitely knew Joe quite well."

"Irish?"

"Well, I'm not sure, but I did hear them mention the Galway Yard a couple of times."

"Interesting," Tiny concluded sipping his Earl Grey from a fine china cup subtlety embellished with the Ascot Racecourse motif. Meanwhile, Rawlings ensured none of the sandwiches or sweet pastry fancies went to waste.

The day's racing continued to its conclusion, and as the evening programme of entertainment commenced, most of which seemed to involve loud music, Tiny decided it was time to leave.

Despite the heavy traffic leaving the ground, they were soon clear of Ascot and safely on their way home. It was a lovely early summer's evening when they arrived back at the Ashbury Estate. The sky was clear, the air still, with just the sound of birdsong to break the silence. The team were already in the yard busing themselves unpacking one of the Land Rovers. The main horsebox containing their fallen star was yet to arrive however just as Tiny and Rawlings was commenting on its absence, it turned through the main gate and slowly made its way down the drive towards the stables. The team of grooms and stable lads seemed to take little notice as the lorry pulled up in the middle of the yard. Ian climbed out from the passenger's side while Paul stopped the engine and remained in the driving seat.

The cab appeared to be specifically designed to seat four. Behind the driver, Gypsy Whistler's groom shuffled across and exited rather inelegantly via the passenger door.

"Where's Joe?" one of the team enquired.

"He's in the back with GW," the groom replied nonchalantly. "He was still a little lively when we loaded, so Joe decided to ride with him."

Tiny later discovered that although technically this was against the rules, not to mention the law, it was apparently common practice on the Ashbury Estate. The team were already moving around to the rear of the horsebox to unlock the tailgate. Another member opened the side door, which was located behind the cab and used to access the area where the horses were loaded.

Rawlings had already headed across to his cottage to change out of his rather uncomfortable formal suit. While Tiny was waiting for him to return, he thought he should try to speak with Ian. Seeing him on his own across the yard, Tiny hadn't moved more than four paces when Ian caught sight of him and purposely turned away. Tiny was perturbed and was about to call out, but before he could say anything, a piercing scream came from the rear of the horsebox stopping everyone in their tracks. For a brief moment, time seemed to stand still; everyone looked around, wondering what was happening. The tranquillity of the perfect summer evening was again shattered as a second scream echoed around the yard, followed by a sense of panic, as everyone started to scrabble around not quite sure what was going on. As more members of the team entered the side door of the horsebox and others scrambled up the ramp at the rear, there were further gasps. Hearing the commotion, Ian turned and headed swiftly towards the horsebox while Paul jumped from the cab and ran round to the rear. Whilst a sense of shock hung in the air, sobbing from several of the team seemed to gaining the upper hand.

"Stand back, let me through!"

Ian took command as he entered the horsebox through the side door.

"Move aside!" Paul cried as he made his way up the ramp before moving along the side of the partitioned area where Gypsy Whistler was tethered.

Tiny moved towards the side door but was prevented from entering by two of the stable team who pushed their way down the steps sobbing intently.

"Oh my goodness!" Tiny heard Ian exclaim. "It's Joe."

Access to the steps eventually became possible and as Tiny entered the horsebox, he saw Ian and Paul standing over Joe, who was lying face down on the floor. A circle of blood surrounded the top half of his body, which was partly covered with straw. The blood pooled around his torso to an area of more than two feet however it had been partly absorbed by sawdust covering the floor. The scene was grim. Ian and Paul stood motionless; neither knew what to do or what to say.

Although Tiny had never actually seen a scene like this, he had heard many descriptions of similar events during his time on the bench, and had seen plenty of photographs.

"Neither of you touch anything," he commanded. "Ian, go and call the police; Paul, move everyone away and cordon off the scene. Nobody else should enter the horsebox until the police arrive."

Ian and Paul remained frozen to the spot.

"Ian, Paul, go now!" Tiny said sharply. Without argument, comment or disagreement, Ian and Paul followed Tiny's command and left the scene.

Tiny stood alone, silently looking at the body on the floor. The ashen grey appearance, the quantity of blood and the eerie stillness seemed to indicate that Joe was dead. Tiny placed his index and middle finger on Joe's ulnar artery to confirm his suspicion. The absence of pulse and coldness to the touch left little doubt.

Standing away from the body, his eyes darted across the scene. Gypsy Whistler did not appear to be injured and remained undeterred, occasionally nibbling on a little hay hanging in a small net on the front of the partitioned area in which he travelled.

Tiny noticed blood smeared on the side of the horsebox by the exit, and then the glint of something shiny caught his eye. Against the bulkhead, partly covered by straw, Tiny glimpsed of what appeared to be a hoof knife covered with blood. As he moved to take a closer look, he heard sirens coming down the drive. Knowing he shouldn't be found trampling all over the crime scene, Tiny exited via the side entrance just as two police cars and an ambulance drew up on either side of the horsebox. The ambulance team quickly entered the trailer, and the police moved everyone back before securing the area. As Tiny stepped away, he noticed a familiar Ford Sierra arriving at the scene just as the medical team left the horsebox. As the senior paramedic solemnly walked down the steps, he gave a little shake of his head to the awaiting police officers; it was clear that Joe was beyond help.

"Hello, Tiny. I had a feeling you might be here," Inspector Stock announced.

"Matthew, always a pleasure to see you although I would prefer if it wasn't under these circumstances."

"Circumstances?"

"Murder, by dear fellow. It's Joe Harrison. someone has stabbed him."

"Really, and you can tell all this from being out here I suppose,"

Before Tiny could answer, a uniformed officer came out of the side door of the horsebox and approached the inspector.

"Excuse me, sir. I think you had better look at this. We have one deceased IC1 male who appears to be in his mid-thirties."

The inspector stood motionless before glaring at Tiny.

"As I say, it's Joe Harrison," Tiny confirmed "and I think you will find the cause of death is a stab wound to the chest from a hoof knife."

"A hoof knife? That's a little specific even for you."

"Well, it's not conclusive however there's one against the bulkhead covered in blood so I would say it's likely, wouldn't you?"

The inspector glared again before accompanying his men into the horsebox. As other more junior officers began unravelling chequered tape around the horsebox, Rawlings came running over from his cottage.

"What's been going on? I heard the sirens. Has someone been injured?"

As Tiny explained the events to Rawlings, the ambulance left the scene only to be replaced by several more police vehicles and a forensic team.

The officers were moving the remaining stable team away from the scene and dividing them up into groups before taking witness statements.

"I think I will head for home," Tiny impatiently concluded, "It's been a long day and there's nothing more I can do here."

"But won't you need to give a statement?" Rawlings asked.

"The inspector knows where to find me." Tiny added before heading towards his Morgan leaving Rawlings at the scene amid the increasing police activity. As Tiny walked away, he knew he was wrong. Of course, he shouldn't be leaving the scene; he was well aware that the first few minutes after the discovery of a crime are the most important and here he was, a key witness, walking away. It was one of those situations that despite realising the error in his behaviour, he continued unabated.

It was around 7.30 pm when Tiny finally arrived back in Oakshaw. As he parked the Morgan and walked across to his house, he reflected on the events of the day and began to regret his decision to leave the traumatic scene at the Ashbury Estate. It was unfair to not allow Inspector Stock to interview him at the time of the incident, and being a key witness, he should have stayed. If truth was told, he found the inspector irritating, and although he was trying to rub along with him as best he could, there were some people that Tiny simply had no patience with. The Inspector was one such person mainly because he was far from convinced that the inspector had any idea what was going on, or any chance of actually of getting to the truth. A typical public servant, he thought to himself, all talk and no grasp on reality. He gave a wry smile as he remembered he had been a public servant himself for more years than he cared to remember.

He was glad to finally change out of his formal morning suit; the novelty of its pomp had long lost its charm. Wearing his comfortable 'gardening' clothes he turned on the wireless before pouring himself a generous measure of Oban 14.

He had just settled in his chair to enjoy the evening concert on the Third, when the telephone rang. With an audible sigh and feeling more than a little annoyed, he jumped up with irritated vigour, turned down the wireless and went into the hall to answer the call.

"Bourne House, Tiny speaking" he announced, trying not to show his irritation.

"Good evening, sir, sorry to bother you. It's Harry."

Chapter Thirteen

It was an unusually chilly dawn that greeted Tiny as he pulled back the curtains. A heavy dew hung on the grass giving a painted form to the thousands of normally invisible cobwebs which now seemed to sparkle with tiny diamonds.

The previous day had been more than a little eventful, and the evening even more so. Tiny had sat in his drawing room long into the night trying to piece matters together. Margaret was due in again to clean and would be expecting an update. He always tried to explain to Margaret the progress he and Rawlings were making however today he was at a loss to know what to say. It seemed the more questions he asked, and the deeper he dug, the more complex matters became. He needed to speak with Rawlings, especially in light of the new information he had received.

Once breakfast was finished, Tiny moved into his study. Deciding it was a respectable hour to call, he picked up the telephone.

"Mr Rawlings, good morning to you, it's Tiny here."

"Oh... good morning, sir. You're up early."

"We need to talk. I have information. Shall we meet for lunch, assuming you are free of course?" Tiny felt it was impolite just to assume but knew in his heart that Rawlings would be free whenever he requested his presence.

They agreed to meet later that day at the Oakshaw Arms for one of Tony's famous bar snacks. Tiny arrived first, and although it was a little early in the day for alcohol, he decided as he wasn't driving, to have his customary bottle of Guinness. Rawlings arrived a few minutes later and looking enviously at the Guinness, added a sparkling mineral water to the tab. After the polite small talk was complete, and once their food had arrived, Tiny turned to more serious matters.

"Harry Metcalf telephoned me last evening."

Rawlings nearly choked on his mineral water causing Tiny to look over the top of his glasses whilst raising an eyebrow.

"Sorry sir, it's the bubbles…"

"Hmm…. really. Anyway, as I was saying, Harry telephoned. He's been asking a few questions, and apparently this operation is bigger than we thought."

He now had Rawlings's full attention and a serious, concerned look gradually engulfed his face.

"How big?"

"Apparently it's managed by a Mexican group accessing cocaine and other drugs from South America. Harry didn't elaborate, but he did mention they were gaining a foothold in London."

"So, Harry knows them?" Rawlings enquired.

"Not exactly. Knows of them I think is more likely. But he did mention one of their key routes is apparently through Ireland."

"Ireland. You mean the Galway Yard?" Rawlings sounded quite excited.

"Steady on, old chap. Harry wasn't that specific, but it does seem to tie up."

"There we are then, that's the connection!" Rawlings declared.

"Maybe, but this is much bigger than we first thought, and Harry warned me against getting involved. Apparently, these chaps aren't the sort of people you want to upset. Anyone who opposes them or gets in their way doesn't seem to live very long." Tiny concluded, adding a touch of drama to heighten the effect.

Rawlings's excitement vanished. "Crikey!" he exclaimed. "Perhaps we had better leave it to the police. We don't want to tangle with those guys."

"We can't give up now," Tiny replied thoughtfully, "but we do need to be careful. This does put matters into a whole new league." He added with sense of concern.

"I'm not so sure, sir. I don't like it. It was okay in the beginning, you know, playing detective, but now, well, it's getting serious."

"Playing detective? Is that what you think we've been doing? Crime is a serious business, and there's some very nasty people around, especially in the world of drugs." Tiny paused before sympathetically adding, "Don't we owe it to Stephen, and now Joe, to find out what's been going on? Surely they deserve justice?"

"I'm not sure, sir, I don't like it..."

"Yes, we've established that," Tiny snapped. "So what do you propose we do, just give up?" He enquired irritably.

"I think we should leave it to the police." Rawlings whispered.

"Fine, if that's what you think. But if you remember, the police still think all that's going on is race fixing, so I don't really have high hopes." Tiny added sarcastically as he rose from his seat.

"I really should be going; the police are calling round this afternoon to take my statement."

With that, Tiny concluded the conversation and briskly walked away leaving Rawlings at the table, more than a little shocked.

After settling the tab, Tiny made his way back to Bourne House, breathing deeply as he tried to calm himself down. Maybe Rawlings was right and he should leave matters to the police. After all, the purpose of leaving London was to seek peace and quiet. Rather than making a nuisance of himself, he should be enjoying country life in his garden, mixing with the community, standing for the parish council perhaps, maybe helping out a charity or two, or sitting on the village fete committee. As his mind strayed, he thought of Rawlings;

161

it wasn't fair to expect him to follow his every move. Just because he had become gripped by this case, it was unreasonable to expect Rawlings to feel the same.

As Tiny reached Bourne House, he was beginning to feel a little guilty especially concerning the brusque manner in which he left his lunch at the pub. Rawlings had become a valued colleague and he had no desire to sour the relationship. Maybe he was becoming a little obsessed? As he pondered this thought, and turned the key in the door, an all too familiar Ford Sierra pulled up outside.

Over compensating for the manner in which he left Rawlings, Tiny welcomed Inspector Stock with an unfamiliar degree of enthusiasm as he invited him warmly into his home. As the inspector settled in the drawing room, Tiny made tea and placed a couple of biscuits and a small cake onto a plate. It was only 2.30, but he thought it just about qualified as time for afternoon tea even though he could still taste his lunch which had barely reached his stomach.

The inspector was in a hurry, and dismissing any attempt of small talk, immediately started on the statement. He was clearly irritated that Tiny had left the scene of Joe's death without seeking permission or making a statement but apart from a couple of barbed remarks he didn't to labour the subject. The point was made and it did not fall on stony ground. Tiny was reluctant to spend much time on something he considered a rather academic and pointless exercise; he was much more interested in finding out how the investigation was progressing. He worked hard to try to change the subject but despite his efforts, the inspector kept changing it back, doggedly pursuing the completion of the statement. Before long, a diatribe of platitudes was ready for signature to which Tiny obediently obliged.

As the inspector returned to his car and drove away, Tiny stood quiet, wondering what Patricia would have thought of the situation. A sudden wave of sadness swept over him, taking him straight back to the loss he had felt at the time of her passing. The house seemed so quiet, the air so still, the world so large. The ticking of the grandfather clock in the hall almost exaggerated the silence as Tiny stood alone pondering his next step. If the police were concentrating on the obvious links to drugs then maybe he would have left it to them, but they still seemed convinced it all centred around race-fixing. This was something Tiny couldn't comprehend, why hadn't they made the connection? It seemed so obvious. Saying that, he hadn't mentioned to the inspector the call he had received from Harry, so maybe it wasn't surprising they were on the wrong track. As Tiny stood motionless, he began to feel weary. It was all getting a little much. He had alienated his colleague, irritated the police and disappointed Margaret; he still had no idea why Stephen died. As the black dog descended, he realised that maybe 'playing detective', as Rawlings called it, wasn't quite as straightforward or as much fun as he first thought.

Early the next day, and nursing a slightly heavy head, Tiny reflected on the conversations he had with Pam and Chuck and of course the untimely death of Joe Harrison. Despondent and unable to see a way forward, he decided to drive over to the Ashbury Estate to tell Chuck that he couldn't really help with any sort of investigation. Now that there had been an actual murder, the police would be all over everything and he really couldn't interfere. His bullish involvement was deflecting valuable police resources from the real issue and he had no intention of inhibiting the inquiry. He needed to tell Chuck of his decision and felt, at the very least, he should speak with him personally to deliver message.

Tiny dropped the roof of the Morgan before setting off. It was not a particularly spectacular day for late June, but he hoped the fresh air would clear his head a little. It didn't. Maybe with hindsight, the generous glass of Oban that followed the Moulin-a-Vent 1982 he enjoyed with his dinner hadn't been such a wise idea.

For the first time since taking delivery of the car, Tiny didn't enjoy the journey. His thoughts were elsewhere and, if truth were told, he was a little worried about the prospect of seeing Rawlings. He wasn't ready to speak with him just yet, but knew that it was he, that needed to make the first move.

In the yard, a single police car was parked next to the horsebox around which crime scene tape still fluttered in the breeze. The young bobby in the drivers' seat suddenly looked interested as Tiny climbed out of his car and looked around intently. Rather than making his way towards the stables, Tiny turned and headed for the main house. No sooner had the PC noticed Tiny walking away, he lost interest, sank back into his seat and assumed his previous semi-conscious state.

Chuck was outside the main door speaking with Ian as the crunch of the gravel beneath Tiny's feet signalled his arrival. Ian glanced in Tiny's direction, but instead of acknowledging his wave of greeting, he slapped Chuck on the shoulder and walked away.

Chuck's attitude couldn't have been more different. Greeting Tiny with warmth and sincerity, he shook his hand and invited him into his home.

"Would you like a sherry, old chap?" he offered.

"It's a little early for me," Tiny replied, still nursing a rather sore head, "but a coffee would be very welcome." As the two men made their way through to the day room, Pam was nowhere to be seen.

"How's your wife?" Tiny enquired. "I hope she hasn't been too upset by what happened?"

"She's in Ireland at the moment, visiting friends," Chuck replied in a rather depressed tone. "Not quite sure when's she back; Ian and the team are over there later in the week so I expect they will all come back together."

That's convenient, Tiny thought settling into his chair. The coffee arrived, and the two men chatted like old friends. Tiny started to relax a little, and as the conversation progressed, he began to feel a little sorry for Chuck.

Chuck was surprisingly open as he explained the pressure his business was currently under. "Technology may be the future, but the expense of development is relentless...," he sighed, "...and as soon as you are ready to present something to the market, it's damn near out of date!"

"And these bloody horses," he continued, "there're costing me a fortune, and what's all this nonsense with drugs, and now a murder? It's about as much as I can take."

Tiny sat quiet. It was clear that Chuck needed to get matters off his chest. As the conversation progressed, Tiny felt humbled. Here he was, worried about his trivial troubles, while sitting in front of him was a man who was under real stress. To make matters worse, Chuck didn't even realise that Pam was being unfaithful especially with someone he obviously considered to be a trusted friend.

Not wishing to add to Chuck's woes, Tiny began to have second thoughts about telling him that he was leaving matters to the police.

Chuck continued. "So, this business with Joe, terrible news. I was shocked. What's going on?"

Tiny decided to be honest with Chuck before informing him of his decision. "Well, the police think there's a race-fixing ring targeting your horses but, in my opinion it's more likely to be about drugs."

"Drugs?"

"Yes, cocaine in particular, and it's probably being imported from your partner's yard in Galway."

Chuck was stunned.

"Apparently it's an organised gang, and it seems likely that Joe was involved."

Although Tiny sounded confident, he was hoping his statement wouldn't prompt too many questions; after all, he didn't actually have a shred of real evidence.

"How do you know all this?" Chuck asked. "You said the police thinks it's to do with race fixing?"

"I still have a few contacts on the shadier side of life who are remarkably well informed," Tiny added tapping the side of his nose as if revealing a real secret.

"I'm not sure which is worse, drugs or race-fixing, but I don't want anything to do with either!" Chuck concluded, sitting back in his chair.

For the first time Tiny began to wonder if Chuck was involved and knew more than he was saying. He hadn't considered this prospect previously which in hindsight, seemed a bit naive if not a little foolish. Was he putting himself in more danger by talking so openly? Chuck seemed genuine, and whist Tiny couldn't be sure, he did pride himself on his ability to judge people. After all, he had made his career staring into the eyes of all those who appeared before him, deciding if they were telling the truth – and that included the accused and the barristers!

"I really think it's a matter for the police," he said.

Chuck placed his cup back on the saucer and laid it on the table. He stared at Tiny.

"You're giving up, aren't you?"

Tiny didn't know what to say.

"Well, not exactly. I just think the police should take the lead. After all they are the professionals." He was beginning to sound like Rawlings, and hated himself for his weakness.

"The police? But you said they weren't even looking into the drugs?"

Chuck had a point and Tiny had no answer.

Chuck continued, "Look, old chap, I can't afford to be caught up in either drugs or race fixing. If the police are looking into race fixing, what's the harm if you continue examining the drugs angle? At least that way both aspects are being investigated?"

Again, Chuck had a point.

"I'm not sure if it's that simple," Tiny responded. "This is organised crime and it's likely that some very undesirable people are involved."

"I'm sure once you have the evidence, the police will follow it up and make the arrests. What do you say?"

Tiny was being boxed into a corner. He was secretly flattered by Chuck's confidence, and felt excited by the prospect of continuing his enquiries. He wasn't normally a man to give up, and Chuck was right: if he was looking into drugs, it really shouldn't interfere with the police investigation. Of course, he didn't really believe this hypothesis but the more he thought about it, the more he managed to convince himself.

"Well, I will probably need to visit the Galway yard if I'm to find out more."

"There's a good chap, quite right, and of course, you should visit Galway. I'm sure the team will be delighted to see you."

Tiny wasn't so sure. Pam was already in Ireland and Ian was due in a couple of days. Of course, Chuck knew nothing of their illicit liaison and besides, it probably had no bearing on the trafficking of drugs anyway Tiny surmised, more as an optimistic wish rather than a realistic assessment.

Promising to provide regular updates, Chuck agreed to make the necessary arrangements and to fund any expenses incurred.

As Tiny left Ashbury Hall and headed back to his Morgan, he strangely felt a sense of relief. Had he made the right decision? Only time would tell however he did feel more focused, his moral compass reset and his purpose renewed. As he approached his car, the young bobby once again popped his head up, grateful for anything of interest in a failing attempt to relieve the boredom. Tiny smiled, climbed into the Morgan and set off up the long drive. Upon reaching the main road, he noticed a black BMW parked just outside the entrance to the estate. A single man in his mid-forties with short grey hair was leaning against the car smoking a cigarette. Tiny gave him a cheery wave not wishing to contravene the country tradition of greeting everyone, even complete strangers. His gesture was suitably ignored with a response of pure puzzlement, leaving him feeling embarrassed and a little deflated.

It was several days later when a crisp white envelope containing a return ticket to Galway dropped onto the mat. Tiny had been weighing up how to approach matters when he arrived in Ireland but if truth was known, he hadn't made much progress. Somehow it didn't feel real, but now he had the tickets in his hand, it all felt very different.

Tiny had decided to leave matters with Rawlings until he returned. He hadn't spoken to him since their fateful lunch more than a week ago. He still didn't know what to say and to be honest, wasn't ready to try.

Rather than driving himself to Bristol airport, Tiny decided take the train. As he still required a lift to the station, he thought he would ask Robert, the local (only) taxi driver, who happened to be Margaret's husband. This would also have the added benefit of raising his reputation with Margaret especially as Robert would undoubtably tell her where he was going.

The flight wasn't until later in the week, and knowing Robert visited the Oakshaw Arms most evenings along with Mike, Trevor and occasional others, he thought he would call into the pub and ask him personally.

Upon entering, and as predicted, the usual suspects were gathered around the bar.

"Evening, Tiny. We hear you're off to Ireland on Thursday."

Tiny was constantly surprised by local gossip; wasn't anything confidential he thought to himself. Saying that, did it really matter? He doubted if any of them knew the real reason why he was going, and even if they did, so what? He had nothing to hide and in fact, a little publicity might shake out a few clues he thought optimistically.

"I take it George will be driving you?"

"Er... no, I've decided to take the train. I'm sure Mr Rawlings has better things to do than run around after me," Tiny added modestly before gently sipping his Guinness.

"You're be needing a lift to the station then?" Robert announced.

Tiny smiled; there was something about village life that he found most satisfying.

Chapter Fourteen

It was an uncharacteristically grey and breezy day, especially for early July. As Robert's taxi rolled to a halt outside of Bourne House, Tiny promptly emerged with bag in hand. Struggling to stop the passenger door from blowing off its hinges, Robert jumped out of his driving seat and ran around to offer Tiny some assistance.

"No need to struggle with that sir, I'll put it in the boot; you just take a seat." Robert was in full taxi driver mode and couldn't do enough to help. Within a few moments, they were on the way to the station, which by car, was less than a thirty minute drive. On route Robert seemed keen to ensure Tiny had first his tickets, second his passport and finally a few Irish pounds, or more correctly, Punts. Tiny felt like a schoolboy being interrogated by his mother but Robert meant well and Tiny certainly wasn't going to embarrass him.

As the taxi pulled into the drop-off zone, Tiny, almost semi-consciously, caught a glimpse of a black BMW parked in the waiting area. The tinted off-side window was only open a few inches which masked the driver but a curl of smoke spiralling from the car betrayed the occupant.

"How much do I owe you?" Tiny enquired.

"No, sir, put your money away. It's been my pleasure. After all you have done for my Margaret, it's the least I can do."

Tiny was taken aback.

Robert continued, "Looking into the death of our Stephen and all that, well, it's really appreciated. You've earned a lot a respect around the village for what you are doing, and well, it hasn't gone unnoticed."

"Thank you, Robert."

Tiny was rarely lost for words but on this occasion, he really couldn't think of anything else to say. As Robert handed him his bag, Tiny decided a handshake was in order.

As he walked towards the station entrance, Robert shouted, "Good luck, sir, and look after yourself!"

The underlying meaning was not lost on Tiny. It seemed clear that no one in the village believed it was a coincidence that Tiny just happened to be visiting Galway. He was embarrassed about his insistence that it was a holiday which now seemed more than a little fanciful. As he boarded the train, embarrassment turned to guilt; maybe in hindsight, he should have been more honest.

The journey was disappointingly easy. Upon reaching Bristol Temple Meads, it was a relatively short hop on the Airport Flyer express bus service, and in a little over forty minutes Tiny was in the airport, checked in and enjoying a swift Campari and soda in the departure lounge. The Aer Lingus flight departed on time with a scheduled duration of barely an hour and a half. In fact, the flight seemed so short, Tiny didn't even have time to complain to the air stewardess about the heavy smoker who was sitting directly behind him, before the aircraft was set for landing.

The Galway yard was located just to the east of Ballyloughane, in an area known as Rosshill. It was a little after two when Tiny left the airport, and being too early to check into his hotel, he decided to travel straight to the yard. Queuing for one of the many taxis parked directly outside the exit, he waited patiently for the attendant to hail the next available cab, before handing his bag to the overly cheerful driver. The journey was a little over fifteen minutes, but still time enough for Tiny to receive the complete history of Ireland, with the convenient omission of the Easter Rising and the ongoing difficulties with the English. As the taxi slowly inched its way through the entrance of Eben Weller Racing, Tiny breathed a quick sigh of relief before being overwhelmed by the opulence of his surroundings. It was different to the Ashbury Estate, much smarter yet similar in many ways.

As he settled his account with the driver, he felt a familiar hand on his shoulder.

"Hello, Tiny. It's lovely to see you here." He turned to see Pam's smiling face lighting up the sky. Before the taxi had pulled away, they were chatting like old friends. Chuck had mentioned that Tiny was visiting and Pam was waiting to greet him, eager to find out more about his investigation. She was horrified to learn of Tiny's theory that cocaine was being smuggled through the yard; she couldn't understand why or how this was happening. Of course, she knew that illegal drugs were becoming a growing concern throughout society, but she really didn't expect it to find it quite so close to home.

"Are you sure about this?" she asked him.

"Well, no, I can't be sure of anything really, but the pieces are beginning to fit together." Tiny replied.

Pam was keen to learn more and suggested he join her for tea. After travelling for most of the day, Tiny was beginning to feel a little weary, so a quiet sit-down and a cup of tea sounded perfect. Pam ushered Tiny towards an impressive house perched on the headland several hundred yards ahead. As they strolled along a beautifully mown path toward the coast, Pam explained that this was one of Eben Weller's many houses, and although he wasn't in Ireland very often, it was available for Pam to stay in whenever she visited. Knowing that Tiny was already booked into the local hotel, Pam made a point of asking him if he would like to stay in the house for the few days he was in Galway. The hollow gesture was not lost on Tiny especially as he knew Ian was also visiting the yard and had no doubt received the same invitation albeit with a different expectation of acceptance.

The house was a large stone property with extensive grounds. It was quite a walk from the yard, albeit not far enough to use a car. As they approached, Tiny noticed that the house wasn't as old as it initially appeared. In addition to the obligatory tennis court, there were several out-buildings including a three-car garage, one closed and two open.

As they drew closer, the grass path eventually gave way to tarmac. Turning the corner towards the front of the house,

Tiny was stopped in his tracks. The view across the estuary towards the Galway Bay golf resort was nothing short of breathtaking.

Although the prospect of tea was attractive, Tiny couldn't resist wanting to see more. Pam was a little reluctant to walk any further and offered to arrange the tea while Tiny enjoyed the view. As the front door closed behind her, he wandered down to the coast and looked out to sea.

Protected by the Aran Islands, Galway Bay is one of nature's natural harbours. With a thriving port in the heart of Galway town only a few miles down the coast, commercial ships from all over the world were regular visitors. As Tiny looked towards the water's edge, distinct scuff marks were visible on the small concrete slipway along with several black rubber wheel marks which led from the water. Turning to look inland, Tiny tried to follow the tracks, which quickly disappeared into the soft shingle. Back at the house, he decided to have a quick look in the outhouses before Pam started to wonder where he was. The closed garage was locked although there was a small gap where the two doors met. Tiny placed his eye against the weathered oak door and peered into the darkness. As his eye adjusted to the light, he could just make out the shape of a galvanised dolly, and behind, the outline of the bow of a rib. In one of the open car-port style garages adjacent, was a Series III soft top Land Rover with a rather tatty khaki hood. Tiny noticed a winch mounted on the front bumper and a tow hitch on the rear. The space next to the Land Rover was empty of vehicles, although rope, fenders and other boating paraphernalia was in abundance.

As Tiny walked across to the house, his mind was in overdrive. A commercial port nearby, a shallow bay, a high-speed rib boat; it all started to add up.

After a very pleasant but uneventful tea, Tiny made his way back to the racing yard. As the day wore on, he became increasingly tired and although he made a point of chatting to most of the stable staff on duty, he hadn't really learnt anything new. In fact, most of them were rather puzzled by his presence and were reluctant to be too cooperative.

Concluding that he was quickly wearing out his welcome, Tiny collected his bag from the yard office, said goodbye to a couple of the grooms who were busy cleaning out the stables, and headed towards the main road. He had spotted signs for The Round Tower hotel as he arrived earlier in the day and knew the walk was fairly short. He was booked in for two nights and was keen to settle in before dinner. As he approached, he became slightly concerned by its appearance which only intensified as he drew closer. It looked more like a pub with rooms rather than a hotel but nevertheless, it was bright, cheerful and looked in reasonable order. Ever the optimist, Tiny hoped appearances were deceptive and that it offered the type of old-fashioned Irish hospitality the country was famous for.

Upon entering the main entrance, He scanned the interior with an analytical eye. The receptionist, spotting what was obviously a new guest, smiled cheerfully before offering Tiny the register. As soon as the paperwork was complete, Cheryl (Tiny had spotted her badge) handed over the key and showed him up to his room. Upon opening the door, he was disappointed by the view over the road. Although he was assured the traffic was minimal especially at night, he was not convinced and wisely, remained sceptical.

The room itself was reasonable. It was light and airy albeit a little tired. The anaglypta wallpaper had seen better days despite suffering several coats of paint, the history of which was clearly displayed along the edges and turned-up corners. Tiny was however impressed by its ensuite shower room, a rarity which was starting to become a popular feature in modern hotels. Unfortunately, being an afterthought, it jutted into the room stealing valuable space and creating a rather an odd shape.

Tiny placed his bag on the folding, chrome baggage-stand before fiddling with the controls of the television. He bounced up and down a couple of times on the overly soft bed before becoming concerned that neighbouring occupants might think he was enjoying himself a little too much. Continuing to look around the room, he considered making himself a cup of tea, that was until he saw the unwrapped bags of Typhoo, sticks of Nescafe and UHT milk jiggers neatly displayed in a rather tired and dusty wicker basket.

After about twenty minutes, he became bored and decided to go in search of dinner. Upon reaching the bar he was greeted by a throng of locals celebrating the end of another working day. Most seemed to be farmers or local tradesmen, but he recognised a few of the crowd from the yard. As he edged towards the bar, the atmosphere was everything he had hoped and probably more than he had expected. Ordering a pint of draught Guinness, which only seemed polite given the circumstances, he was handed a menu. Not bothering to use his glasses, he squinted at the choice before him and spotted a Beef and Ale pie which sounded quite appealing. Quickly placing his order, he moved away from the bar to find a table.

Tiny had only been seated for a couple of minutes before one of the locals sat himself down on the neighbouring chair.

"You're that chap from England aren't you; the one who's been nosing around the yard."

The tone was bordering upon threatening and it made Tiny uneasy.

"I'm just here for a few days to visit my friend Pam Stern." Tiny responded calmly.

"So you're not poking around the yard then?"

"Like I said, I'm just here for a few days visiting my friend. Now if you would excuse me, I think my dinner just about to arrive."

With that, the man stood up and merged back into the throng of locals stood at the bar.

Tiny had never been so thankful to see a waitress bearing what disappointingly turned out to be a fairly ordinary pub supper. He was not used to being challenged by a complete stranger and was unnerved by the event. Looking around the room, it was clear that he was drawing attention. The majority of the occupants appeared to be local, but at the end of the bar Tiny spotted a lone individual, smoking a cigarette, and failing miserably at trying not to be noticed. Everyone else seemed to be in groups; some were looking in

Tiny's direction and some were not, however they were all chatting and laughing and taking little notice, all that is, except this thick-set, grey-haired, middle-aged man. As Tiny looked over, he turned his back and once again faced the bar. Tiny was disturbed; the man seemed to look vaguely familiar but he couldn't remember where, or even if, he had seen him before. He wished Rawlings had accompanied him and regretted the silly disagreement they had the previous week. In hindsight, Rawlings was correct; this was getting out of hand. Perhaps he should have left matters to the police, especially after Joe's murder.

Quickly finishing his supper, Tiny deciding to skip dessert and made his way back to his room. He had a good book awaiting him, a bottle of Bushmills, duty free of course, and his portable wireless for company. As he left the bar, it was apparent that he was still attracting attention. In addition to the thick set, middle-aged man who took such an interest earlier, there now appeared to be a taller, younger man watching his movements. Tiny hurried to his room securely locking the door behind him. As he drew the curtains, he noticed a dark car parked opposite, a familiar curl of smoke was rising from the small gap in the driver's door window. Was he being followed, or was being alone in a foreign country leading to a little paranoia?

Any hopes that he had for a quiet evening were quickly thwarted, mainly due to the noise emitting from the bar, which combined with the constant sound of traffic racing by seemed to stretch long into the early hours. Ireland might be famous for its hospitality but at that moment, all Tiny really wanted was a little peace and quiet.

A restless night was thankfully followed by gloriously peaceful morning, and a rather enjoyable full Irish breakfast. Tucking away the last slice of toast, which he wanted more than needed, Tiny decided to visit the main town before heading back to the yard. The hotel kindly organised a taxi and before long, Tiny found himself wandering the streets of Galway.

It was still only a little after 10.00 am but the town seemed to be bustling with office workers, tradesmen and shoppers. Struggling to find his bearings, Tiny noticed a man standing on the opposite side of the road just staring. Was it the same man as the previous evening?

Wandering aimlessly, Tiny was keen to feel the rhythm of the town through his shoes. Purposely taking the occasional side alley, Tiny was impressed with the variety of independent shops, cafes and restaurants. Unlike some of the major British towns, this beautiful coastal resort hadn't yet been corrupted by the growing dominance of the major High Street brands.

Although it wasn't in the centre, the port seemed to be the heart of the town. Even though it was more of a commercial area, and well off the beaten track for tourists, Tiny decided to explore. Making an excuse here and there to chat with some of the dock workers, he discovered the impressive breadth of products imported into Galway. Shipments were received from all around the globe which were matched, albeit not equally, by a healthy volume of goods exported. Recalling his conversation with Harry, Tiny was especially interested to learn that regular shipments arrived from Mexico, Nicaragua, Venezuela and in particular, Colombia.

181

After walking for more than two hours Tiny was feeling tired, something he firmly attributed to the sea air rather than his advancing years. Wandering back to the main shopping district, he found a café to rest his weary legs. Ordering what turned out to be a rather excellent cup of black coffee, and a Danish pastry which he doubted had ever seen Denmark, he sat quietly and began to digest what he had learnt. As he peered out the window in deep thought, he spotted the shadowy silhouette of a man paused on the opposite side of the road. Coincidence, he wondered, or was that the same man he saw earlier? As he pondered this dilemma, his thoughts were shattered by the opening of the café door. A thick-set middle-aged man with a blank expression slowly walked in and sat quietly in a corner seat. He immediately lit a cigarette as he observed life on the street outside. Tiny was now in no doubt; he was being followed which he concluded could mean one of two things: either he was starting to make progress or he was in danger. His heat sank as reality hit and he suddenly realised it could actually mean both.

During the chats he had with the dock workers, Tiny had discovered that ships docked at all hours of the day and night dependent upon the tide. In hindsight, he now thought, that was rather obvious, but Tiny was still fascinated by the volume of trade moving through the port and how it was organised on such an industrial scale. Having blagged a copy of the manifest for today's arrivals, Tiny took it out and laid it on the table before him. A ship called the Ocean Star from Puerto Bolivar was due in just after 8.00 pm that evening. It was listed as carrying coffee, tobacco and bananas, and though he had no reason to doubt that, he thought he might just take a look as it arrived. After feeling refreshed, and with time to spare, Tiny decided he would walk back to the stables rather than taking a taxi. Now that he had a better idea of the layout of the town, he realised the coastal path was easily accessible and according to the café owner, it was only a little over two miles back to the stable yard. Besides, it was a beautiful day, and he was promised the path offered spectacular views across the bay. He was not disappointed by the walk. The coastal path rose high above the gently lapping shoreline, and being well trodden, made for easy progress. Apart from a couple of cyclists, the path was virtually deserted which made the views seem even more spectacular. As Tiny paused to catch his breath, he spotted a lone man several hundred yards behind him. He decided to ignore him, and after a little over an hour, the stable yard came into view along with the house where Pam was staying. Wondering whether he should check if Pam was at home, he decided that perhaps it wouldn't be appropriate and so went directly to the stables.

After a rather uneventful afternoon wandering around the yard, Tiny thought he would take the coastal path once more and head back into town for a little supper before the Ocean Star docked. He could easily take a taxi directly back to the hotel later when he was ready to leave. Time was pressing on; it was already after 6.30 pm however just as he was leaving the stables, he noticed Ian walking across towards the yard from the direction of the house.

"Ian, my dear chap, how are you?"

"Ah, Tiny, good to see you." Ian looked more than a little sheepish. "Pam mentioned that you were visiting. On holiday I believe?"

"Well… yes indeed, just a few days away you know, a little see air and a change of scenery. Is Pam around?" Tiny added teasingly, knowing only too well where she would be.

"Not sure," Ian replied vaguely, "I suppose you could try the house?"

With a brief nod, Ian walked towards the office, denying Tiny the opportunity to ask any further questions. Of course, he didn't really need to see Pam… but it might be useful… but then again, if he didn't hurry, he would miss the arrival of the Ocean Star. As he stood alone, and torn with indecision, a faint buzzing sound was just about detectable. As he moved his head first to the right, and then the left trying to ascertain the direction where the buzzing was coming from, a groom came out of one of the stables pushing a wheelbarrow.

"Excuse me," Tiny asked, "what's that noise?"

"What noise?" the groom replied most unhelpfully before wandering off.

Calculating that the design of the stables was probably reflecting the sound, (he was well familiar with the principle of William Tucker's acoustic mirrors at Dungeness) he slowly walked away from the yard and towards the coastal path. Gently placing each foot on the track as silently as possible, the buzzing was becoming more distinct yet seemed to be moving farther away. Still some fifty yards from the cliff edge, Tiny peered across the bay, his eye drawn to the diminishing wake of a small craft. In the distance, he could just make out a speedboat bouncing across the waves as it left the calmness of the bay and turned around the headland before heading out to sea.

In the distance, a large container ship dominated the horizon. It was now 7.15 pm, and looking at his watch, Tiny concluded that this was likely to be the Ocean Star.

He hurried along the coastal path, hoping to arrive at the harbour edge before the Ocean Star berthed. About halfway, the path finally curled around the cliffs allowing a clear view of the port. The Ocean Star could now be seen in all its glory. Two tugs were attached to the front with another behind, guiding it carefully into the port. Realising just how slowly matters were progressing, Tiny was thankful to be able to ease off the pace. As he paused to catch his breath, he again noticed a speedboat, this time returning to the calm waters of the bay. Of course, he couldn't be sure it was the same one as he spotted earlier but for some reason, he couldn't take his eyes off it as it bounced across the water, the engine note rising and falling as each wave was conquered.

Concluding that the Ocean Star would probably take a while before it finally docked, Tiny continued to watch the speedboat as it made its way across the bay and towards Rosshill. As the boat drew closer, Tiny saw it was actually a rib, with two persons on board. In the rear of the boat were several large packages, which appeared to be wrapped in plastic. Tiny was transfixed by the scene that stretched out before him. He quickly decided that this boat was more

185

interesting than the Ocean Star, especially as it seemed to be heading back towards the area where the stables were located. Tiny turned and started to walk back along the path before noticing a lone man standing motionless several hundred yards ahead. Spotting Tiny approaching, the man immediately turned and started to walk back in the same direction adding to Tiny's theory that he was being followed. He had been so busy watching the speedboat and the Ocean Star that he hadn't really paid attention to who else was on the path. It was now clear that he was not on his own.

Despite walking as quickly as he could, he wasn't able to get close enough to confirm the identity of the man who was steadily vanishing into the horizon. Perhaps it was the grey-haired man he had seen the previous evening, or maybe the younger, thinner one he had seen earlier in the town? It was a puzzle, but he was too busy to dwell. By the time he arrived at the house where Pam was staying, the boat had also disappeared. Although he had no business being there, he decided to have a quick look around the garage and outhouses especially remembering his previous observations. As before the garage was locked with the Land Rover parked nearby. He cast his eye towards the shoreline, where two wet tracks across the shingle were clearly visible. Tiny walked towards the Land Rover and placing his hand upon the bonnet, felt the warmth of recent use. Pausing for a moment to let events sink in, his attention was suddenly drawn towards the house. A flutter of the curtains on the upper landing caught his eye followed by a brief glimpse of Pam, wearing a black negligee, staring in his direction, her flowing hair draped across her shoulders. As soon as she noticed him looking, she was gone, the swaying curtains the only evidence of her existence.

As he walked back towards the hotel, Tiny's thoughts were in turmoil. It looked very much as if the boat had probably travelled out to meet the Ocean Star to collect the plastic-wrapped packages, which were probably dropped overboard. It seemed likely that the rib he had seen locked in the garage was the boat in question, and that pointed to the yard being involved. And what about Pam? Was she involved too? How much did she know? And was she covering for someone? The questions continued to spin around Tiny's head all the way back to the hotel. As he walked the short distance along the pavement towards the front door, the silhouette of a young, skinny man was clearly visible lurking in the shadows on the opposite side of the road. It was now 8.45 pm; Tiny was tired and hungry and didn't have the energy or courage to challenge anyone. He entered the hotel and headed straight for the main bar which being depressingly lively, did not fill Tiny's heart with glee. Choosing a corner table, judging it to be one of the quietest available, Tiny hung his jacket over the back of the chair and headed for the bar. After ordering a fish supper, along with a pint of Guinness, he returned to his table hoping he wasn't going to suffer a repeat of the previous evening.

Oblivious to his surroundings, especially the now familiar grey-haired man who sat at the bar smoking a cigarette, Tiny tucked into his rather tasty supper in relative peace. Were standards improving or was it just because he was hungrier than normal? The jury was still out however just as he was finishing the last mouthful, a shout pierced the drone in the bar.

"Tiny, hello there!"

Tiny turned around and was greeted by the most surprising sight. In the middle of the bar stood Chuck dressed in a very smart three-piece beige lounge suit, clutching a bouquet of red roses.

"Chuck, my dear fellow, what are you doing here?"

"I thought I would surprise Pam; it's our wedding anniversary tomorrow and well, why not!"

"That's very romantic of you," Tiny responded, even more surprised.

"Well, she's always saying I'm not spontaneous, so I thought I would show her! I'm just off over to the house now, wish me luck!"

Chuck was very upbeat, which unsettled Tiny ever further. Cupping his hand to the side of his mouth as if a secret was forthcoming, Chuck unsubtly whispered, "Let's catch up tomorrow. I want to hear all about your investigation."

Before Tiny could respond, Chuck was gone, parting the crowd before him which quickly refilled the void left in his wake. Tiny knew that Pam was in the house, and prayed that she was alone. He had grown to quite like Chuck and despite the way Pam had described him, didn't wish him any harm. Tiny was touched by his youthful impulsive gesture to his wife which he feared wouldn't be taken in the spirit in which it was meant.

Deciding there was nothing more he could do to help protect Pam from her probable fate, Tiny retired to his bed.

Chapter Fifteen

It was a dull and cloudy morning as Tiny finished his breakfast. After packing his belongings, he checked out of the hotel deciding to travel directly to the airport from the stable yard. He was looking forward to going home and if truth was told, he was glad to see the back of The Round Tower Hotel. He had received far more attention that he expected or sought, and was worried by the shadowy figure who was obviously interested in his activities. And how about the thick-set, middle aged smoker who seemed to be everywhere? Was that a coincidence? Tiny had moved way beyond coincidence and was beginning to see conspiracy everywhere he looked. He was aware that locals tended to stick together, but he had hoped he would have been made to feel a little more welcome. So much for that traditional Irish hospitality, he thought.

Tiny was becoming familiar with the short walk to the stables and within minutes the yard was within sight. The area around the stables was a hive of activity; the local blacksmith was busy shoeing one of the horses with a further two awaiting their turn. A lone man was stood to one side casually taking in the scene whilst missing nothing. As Tiny paused to watch the activities laid out before him, he noticed Chuck marching down the path from the house; he did not look happy. As Chuck approached, he almost swept Tiny off of his feet as he ushered him into the office before swiftly closed the door. Tiny feared the worst.

He was right to be worried. Being so far from home, it was obvious Chuck needed to speak to someone. Little response was needed as he poured his heart out as Tiny remained expressionless. His anger swelled into a crescendo of bitterness and disbelief as he described how he caught Pam and Ian together. He described the heated argument which had ensued with Pam, quickly followed by an altercation with Ian. Tiny really didn't know how to respond but given the size of Chuck, he guessed that Ian didn't fare too well. He wasn't good at giving advice, and felt embarrassed about trying to sympathise, so he sat quietly until Chuck stopped talking. He stared at Tiny with thunder in his eyes.

"Did you know?" he demanded.

"My goodness no... I had no idea." Tiny replied trying hard to sound convincing. He hated lying; in fact, his whole career had relied upon people telling the truth. But a little white one, to spare someone's feelings, and perhaps his own health, he regarded as acceptable.

Chuck sank down into one of the chairs, his head in his hands. After a few moments of silence, he looked up. "Enough of my troubles. What did you find out? Are drugs coming into the yard?" His voice was hard and cold, stripped of emotion.

Tiny needed to be straight with Chuck; and although he was having a stressful day, he deserved to know the truth.

"Yes, I'm sorry to say, I think they are. I don't know who's involved yet but I suspect shipments are being transferred at sea into a speedboat and brought ashore close to the house. I'm not sure where they are stored or where they go after that."

"Oh my goodness, that's all I need," Chuck replied, dropping his head back into his hands.

"I also think I'm being followed."

"My poor chap; it wasn't my intention to put you in danger."

"I know," Tiny responded with a quiet smile. "It's okay, really it is, I'm sure I'll be fine."

"I need to get back to the Ashbury Estate," Chuck concluded rising to his feet.

"I'm sorry, truly I am," Tiny whispered solemnly.

"Nonsense, none of this is your fault, and I appreciate you finding out about the drugs. It appears I have no idea what's happening right under my own nose!"

It was obvious Chuck was not merely referring to the drugs. As he placed his hand on Tiny's shoulder, he calmly muttered, "You're a good friend. I know this hasn't been easy for you, but I knew if anyone could find out what was going on, it would be you, and I was right, wasn't I?

You're welcome," Tiny replied. "I'm sorry I didn't have better news."

Chuck gave a wry smile, and with a nod of his head, he was gone. Tiny stood alone trying to make sense of the last few minutes. He felt sorry for Chuck, not only regarding Pam, but also the situation with the drugs – assuming of course, he didn't already know. Tiny was normally good at seeing through people and assessing whether they were telling the truth, but on this occasion he really wasn't sure. He stood quiet, peering out across the yard. The scene that stretched before him made the day seemed so normal, yet it wasn't.

The silence was broken by the door being suddenly opened.

"Hello squire." The blacksmith uttered touching his cap as he entered the office.

His sarcastic tone made Tiny bristle. "Can I be of any assistance?" he asked coolly.

The blacksmith just smiled and started to chat about his work, family and life in general. Tiny was rarely surprised by people but was quite taken aback by such innocent friendship. He started to warm to the man and soon began to appreciate his mischievous sense of humour. Finally, here was the type of Irishman he was expecting.

Quickly discovering that the blacksmith worked for most of the local yards, and seemed to know everyone who had anything to do with horses, Tiny felt this was his opportunity to find out what was going on. As he probed a little deeper, he desperately tried to find a way bring the conversation around to drugs.

"So, you'll be wanting to know about the drugs then?" the blacksmith enquired. Tiny was stopped in his tracks. Did he make it that obvious?

"Well, I did hear a rumour." Tiny replied, trying to sound vague.

"Ah... you heard more than that, so you did."

"Well..."

"I'll tell you what I do know. Yes, there is talk around the yards, and yes, I know it goes on. There are so many horses moving all over the place, it's difficult for the authorities to check, you see."

"But how do they do it?"

"It's inside the horses, in little parcels. Passes straight through, you see. Easy!"

Tiny was stunned, partly by the information, but mainly by the everyday nature in which it was delivered. It was like normal life, as if everyone was doing the same. Tiny was speechless trying hard to dismiss the matter with a false sense of unimportance.

"One more thing: who's that skinny man with blond hair who's been hanging around the yard? I've seen him a few times while I've been here."

The blacksmith's expression instantly became solemn. "You don't want to be messing with him, so you don't. Best you give him a wide berth if you catch my drift!" He added giving Tiny a nervous wink.

Making an excuse that he was too busy to chat anymore, the blacksmith bade Tiny farewell, left the office and continued about his business. Tiny stood alone; his stomach turned and his heart raced as the reality of the situation finally became clear. Still having the card for the taxi in his pocket he received when he arrived, Tiny decided it was time to head for the airport. Picking up the office telephone he arranged for the same driver to collect him as soon as possible. It was a little early for his flight, but he thought he would be safer at the airport and maybe he would relax more than if he stayed around the yard. There was no further need to chat to the stable lads and under the circumstances, he would prefer not to meet Pam and certainly not Ian; and as for the suspicious character outside, the least said the better.

It was clear that his presence was attracting unwelcome attention, and any thought of innocent adventure had suddenly been replaced by an unsettling sense of fear. It was worrying to think that he was being followed, especially since there now appeared to be more than one person interested in his activities. His sense of tension had increased considerably, and feeling more than a little awkward, Tiny decided it was definitely time to head for home!

Chapter Sixteen

"Oh, who can that be?" Tiny irritably muttered out loud.

He hadn't been home more than thirty minutes when there was a knock at the door. Slightly irritated, Tiny made his way from the sitting room to the hall. He was looking forward to a quiet evening, the concert on the Third, a large measure of Oban 14, (he considered he had earned it) and his comfy armchair; he did not appreciate being disturbed.

Opening the front door, Tiny was rather taken aback.

"Alan! This is a surprise. Come in."

"Good evening, sir, sorry to disturb you."

"Not at all, it's good to see you. I was just pouring myself a little scotch if you fancy one?"

"Perhaps just a small one, since you're having one yourself."

The two old colleagues sat down opposite each other. It did not seem possible to imagine anything evil in such an idyllic village setting, but Tiny had a feeling that was about to change.

"You have been creating quite a stir. I thought we had agreed you would leave matters to us?"

"No, I think you will find that it was you who decided that I should leave matters to you," Tiny fired back. "and where did that get us? Inspector Stock seemed determined to think it was all about race fixing!" Tiny added with unfamiliar gusto.

"Ah, yes, well… we've moved on from there." Alan admitted in a much more conciliatory tone.

"I should think so. As I believe I mentioned the last time we spoke, it's the import, sale and distribution of cocaine that's at the heart of this case," Tiny announced haughtily although he swiftly regretted his self-important tone. He had a great deal of respect for Alan and needed to keep him on his side.

"Look, Alan," he said appeasingly, "you are a good detective, you have a nose for these things."

"I'm the Assistant Chief Constable, I'm not close to the day-to-day detail."

"In your heart you will always be a detective whatever rank you hold. You're a natural, it's in your blood."

Alan sat back in his chair and slowly sipped his whisky, looking wistful. For a moment, silence reigned and peace was once again restored.

In what seemed like an age, the tranquillity of the setting was suddenly broken.

"I hear you went to Ireland? Caused quite a stir there too."

"Well, you should know; I take it is was your chap that was following me around?" Tiny proclaimed with an unfamiliar degree of arrogance.

197

Alan looked puzzled. "No," he said. "Why would we be following you?"

The colour drained from Tiny's face; his arrogance instantly evaporated being swiftly replaced with a sickening sense of unease. Both Alan and Tiny were all too well aware what this meant: someone else had been following Tiny. But who? Both sat back in their chairs concentrating upon their whisky quietly reflecting upon the situation.

"Of course, we know all about the cocaine." Alan announced with a degree of self-importance. "We've known for some time."

"So why all the pretence about race fixing?" Tiny asked feeling rather confused.

"Well, when I say 'we', I don't mean the local team. This is being managed at a much higher level."

"I'm not sure whether I should be worried or reassured," Tiny responded.

Alan stared disapprovingly. "Look, you have one of the sharpest legal minds I've ever known, and yes, you were right about the cocaine, but you really should leave this to us. I'm serious; these aren't people you should be messing around with, and as you've just pointed out, you are probably already being followed."

"I appreciate your concern, but I've come too far to let this go. I made a promise and intend to see it through."

"You're a stubborn old coot." Alan rose from his chair. "I'm not surprised to hear that, but you need to be careful." Tiny showed Alan to the door, and was once again, he left alone with his thoughts. If truth was told, the situation did worry him. There was a time in Ireland when worry had grown into fear, and as for the acquisition of being stubborn, well, maybe Alan had a point. It was easy to be brave in your own home, but the real world outside was a different matter.

A sleepless night followed.

Recently, Tiny had been waking in the morning thinking about the case. More lately, this had been replaced by waking during the night, and this night was probably the worse yet. Although another day had just about dawned, he still felt exhausted. Was it just the worry, or did he overdo matters a little when he was in Ireland? Whatever the cause, he knew he viewed matters more pessimistically when he was tired however the sheer magnitude of this   case   was beginning to take its toll.

Of course, Alan was probably right, but he knew he would feel guilty if he stopped. Tiny thought back to his service with the RAF and remembered a quote from Winston Churchill: *'Success is not final; failure is not fatal: it is the courage to continue that counts.'* He needed now more than ever to muster the courage to see this through to the end, but he couldn't do it alone. He had to bring Rawlings back on side; his help was essential, if only as someone with whom to discuss the next move. Rather than making a point of seeking him out, Tiny decided the best approach was to just 'bump' into him, probably while on the Ashbury Estate.

It was a little after nine; and Tiny knew the lads would still be out on the gallops exercising the horses. With a little time on his hands, he decided to wander over to the village shop and pick up a copy of the Times.

The familiar 'ting' of the door rang out as Tiny entered the shop. Trevor was busy behind the counter restocking the tobacco display.

"Good morning, Trevor, a copy of The Times if you would be so kind."

"Good morning to you, sir. You know I would be happy to deliver; you only have to ask." Tiny appreciated the kind offer which Trevor made every time, but he still enjoyed the personal approach. Besides, there wasn't really much effort involved walking across the green and for some strange reason, he felt less committed making his own arrangements. As Tiny and Trevor shared polite niceties, his eyes caught the headline on the front page.

DRUG RAIDS ACROSS LONDON; 14 ARRESTED – FULL STORY PAGE 5.

Making his excuses to Trevor, Tiny hurried back to his cottage. He sat quietly at his kitchen table, turned to page five and read intently about the coordinated raids on several addresses across London. Although no names were mentioned, naturally his thoughts turned to Harry. Despite Harry's criminal past, and questionable present, he didn't wish him any harm and hoped he wasn't involved.

Looking at the clock, Tiny decided it was a decent sort of time to make his way to the estate. Although it was a glorious July day with near perfect weather, Tiny was in no mood to drop the hood of the Morgan. As he left the confines of the village and breathed in the stillness of a summer's day, he noticed a familiar black BMW some distance behind him. Keeping a close eye, the car continued to follow despite several detours including a double circuit of a roundabout.

Upon arriving at the Ashbury Estate, Tiny was unnerved to see the black BMW park at the entrance although the occupant appeared reluctant to leave the car. The trademark thin curl of smoke once again drifted from the driver's dark tinted window, which was open no more than three inches.

Tiny considered approaching the driver, but having never been one for conflict, his mind worked hard to justify the several reasons why it probably wouldn't be a good idea. Having convinced himself to leave well alone, he wandered towards the stables, where a hive of activity was underway. The horses had long since returned from their morning exercise and were in the midst of being fed and groomed. Paul Chipping caught sight of Tiny, and promptly turned his back and disappeared deep into the tack store. Ian was also around, and although he nodded in Tiny's direction, it was clear that he didn't really want to speak.

Tiny was beginning to feel ostracised. He hadn't realised that asking a few questions would cause such animosity. As he paused and looked around, he caught sight of Rawlings astride a ride-on mower. Not convinced he would receive any different treatment from him, he smiled in his direction and awaited a response. Thankfully Rawlings stopped the mower and walked across the yard to speak.

Tiny took the initiative. "Good morning, Mr Rawlings, how nice to see you."

"You too sir," Rawlings responded a little sheepishly. "How did the trip to Ireland go?"

"Well, it was very interesting. Let me tell you all about it; how about some tea?"

That was all that was needed to put them back on an even keel. Neither mentioned the previous disagreement, neither needed too, words were not necessary, their body language was apology enough.

As they gently strolled away from the yard, Rawlings enquired, "Did you catch up with that chap?"

"Which chap?" Tiny replied.

There was a man here earlier asking after you."

"Oh, you mean the man in the black BMW; the one that's parked at the end of the drive," Tiny exclaimed in a knowing sort of way.

Rawlings looked puzzled. "No, the Irishman, in the blue Vauxhall Cavalier."

"Irishman? You mean a thick set man with grey hair?" Tiny persisted.

"No, a skinny chap with blond hair. He definitely had an Irish accent."

Tiny's blood ran cold.

"And what's this about a BMW?" Rawlings enquired.

"We have much to discuss," Tiny concluded as Rawlings opened the front gate to his cottage.

Over tea, Tiny brought Rawlings up to speed with the proceedings in Ireland. He described the events in the hotel, and how Chuck had caught Ian and Pam together. He mentioned the cocaine route from South America, and how the smugglers transferred the drugs from the ship, how the yard was involved and how they smuggled the drugs into the UK using the horses.

"Puts a whole new meaning to the term drugs mule!" Rawlings exclaimed, as if he was the first one to think of it.

Tiny just frowned, before continuing.

Rawlings took matters more seriously when Tiny described how he had been followed from the UK by the man in the BMW. The atmosphere turned even more tense when Tiny mentioned the advice received from the blacksmith regarding the blond-haired Irishman. An awkward silence filled the room as both men sipped their tea.

"Look like you've stirred up a hornet's nest," Rawlings commented trying to summarise the conversation.

"Well, there doesn't look like there's going to be any winners." Tiny concluded with a sigh. "Two men from The Ashbury Estate dead, a serious accident at Newbury, a jockey killed - obviously now drug related, plus a broken marriage," he continued.

"And the two men following you," Rawlings added.

"Indeed, with undoubtably less than honourable intentions if I were to guess," Tiny surmised modestly.

"Surely the police must be able to help?"

"Well, the senior guys probably know more than they are saying, but I doubt if the local mob know much. They certainly don't seem to be aware of the two men following me, that's for sure."

"What are we going to do?" Rawlings asked.

"That's a good question. I suggest you keep your ear to the ground while I go and speak with Chuck about the cocaine racket. Hopefully he's calmed down a little by now." Tiny rose from his chair ready to leave. The two colleagues briefly paused before going their separate ways. Rawlings returned back to the yard to continue with his grass mowing, while Tiny headed towards the house.

Chapter Seventeen

Ashbury Hall somehow felt different. It was as if its very soul had been stripped from the walls and all that was left was an empty shell, mere protection from the elements rather than a home. Chuck was pleased to see Tiny, and was as polite as ever, though it was clear his thoughts were elsewhere. He ushered Tiny through to the drawing room before offering coffee. He then promptly left the room to presumably to make it himself. Tiny stood alone, feeling slightly awkward. After a few minutes Chuck reappeared clutching a tray containing two cups of coffee and a packet of digestive biscuits still in their wrapping. It was quite a pathetic sight: Chuck struggling with the door trying to keep up the pretence of normality.

Tiny went to the rescue. "Let me help you, old chap."

"No, it's okay, I have it," Chuck insisted waving Tiny into a seat.

"Are you on your own today?" Tiny enquired.

Chuck explained that Pam was staying with friends at the moment, although he wasn't quite sure with whom or where. The household staff were all on holiday pending redundancy, which would be finalised when the house and estate were sold.

"Sold? So you are selling up?"

"Yes, I've had enough. It's not the same anymore. It's been nothing but trouble since I bought it and it's costing me a fortune."

"I see... I'm very sorry to hear that."

"And, you will never guess, Pam's divorcing me! Seriously, I received the papers yesterday... can you believe it!"

"Divorcing you? That's all a little sudden isn't it?"

"Well, I think she and that rat Ian have been planning this for a while. Just biding their time until they were ready. I think my visit to Ireland brought matters forward a little."

"But on what grounds is she divorcing you?"

"Well, you wouldn't believe it: unreasonable behaviour, apparently!"

"Unreasonable behaviour? That seems a little strange given the circumstances. Did she not mention her own adultery?"

"Nope, not a peep. Apparently, I have been spending too long away from the marital home. And I opened her post, and I spoilt her last birthday – you know, the party I put on during Ascot."

"I'm sorry, I'm not sure if I understand. You opened her post?

"Well, I opened one letter from the bank which I thought was mine. I didn't see her name through the window in the envelope. Anyway, it turns out that Pam had opened a private account and was siphoning off money from the business. Outrageous! And you should see how much is in there! I tell you; they have been planning this for quite a while."

"Spoilt her party? What party?"

"Oh, I arranged a party for her 50th birthday during Ascot week at that country house hotel just outside Winchester. It was only for her family and friends. Cost me a fortune, I thought it would be a real treat for her."

"So what was the problem?"

"No idea, it was a fabulous day but apparently according to the divorce application, I spoilt what should have been 'a momentous and special occasion'! Talk about looking for excuses"

Chuck's pain was clear to see.

"I'm sorry old chap, I really don't know what to say," Tiny sympathised. whilst his own thoughts drifted to the long, happy years he had spent with his beloved Patricia.

Chuck continued, "I only bought this estate for her; I could barely afford it. Had to work all hour's day and night just to keep my head above water, and for what?"

Chuck had moved on from merely relaying his news to venting his frustration, grateful for someone to talk to. Tiny sat awkwardly, quietly listening while the poor man emptied his soul to someone he barely knew.

Tiny was humbled.

"Well, there you have it; that's about all I can say." Chuck sighed as he sank into his armchair.

"It will get better old chap; I promise you." Tiny replied. "You may not think it now, but see this as a chapter that's closing. A new one, and a much happier one, will be ahead."

"I was quite happy with the chapter I had," Chuck whispered, a tear appearing in his eye.

"Anyway, I suppose it is what it is. I'm off back to my flat in London next week. I no longer want to be here, especially if Pam decides to return."

"Is there any prospect of that?"

"Oh yes, apparently she planning to return next week, but I really can't face her. It's probably better if I'm out of the way."

"And what about the police enquiry?" Tiny judged that Chuck was calm enough to turn the conversation around.

"The police enquiry? Oh, you mean the drugs."

"Yes indeed. We know the yard's involved; cocaine is being smuggled in via the horses direct from Galway. It's off-loaded from ships coming in from Columbia."

"What do you mean, via the horses? Is it concealed in the trailers during transport?" Chuck looked puzzled.

"No, the drugs are inside the horses"

"In the horses?" Chuck enquired.

"Apparently so. That would account for the strange behaviour of the horse that killed Stephen, and for the incident at Newbury."

"Yes, I suppose so... But how about Joe Harrison? Who killed him?"

"Ah, I'm not sure about that at the moment however matters are beginning to make a little more sense." Tiny concluded thoughtfully.

"I never did trust Eben Weller. I always wondered why he was so keen to strike up the partnership between our two yards. He's a snake!"

Tiny was taken aback. "You think Eben's behind this?"

"Well, I did wonder. He has a reputation for high spending, but from what I can see his business is built on straw. You have to ask where the money comes from. Not that I listen to rumours, you understand."

"No, indeed. I do understand." Tiny was impressed, not only by how astute Chuck was at business, but also how good he was at reading people. His psychological radar was obvious still working, with everyone of course, apart from his nearest and dearest. Maybe this was why Chuck was so upset. Maybe he should have seen it coming, but as they say, the husband is always the last to know.

"You say Pam is due back sometime next week?" Tiny asked trying to change the subject.

"Well, so she says. I can't say we have much contact at the moment. I won't be here anyway. As I've said, I'm off back to

London later today." There was no more to be said, so Tiny rose from his chair, wished Chuck well and headed for the door.

As Tiny was leaving the house, they shook hands. "It's been a pleasure knowing you, Tiny. Thanks for all your help, and well... you know..."

"You're welcome, and please stay in touch."

Chuck looked defeated. "I really can't thank you enough."

"It will get better, I promise you." Tiny added sympathetically without any certainty as to the future. Platitudes were easy at times like this, but although Tiny knew he sounded a little shallow, he didn't really know what else to say.

From his conversation, he was now convinced that in the business of cocaine smuggling, Chuck was an innocent bystander. He had laid bare his soul, and if he had been involved, Tiny felt sure he would have known. He prided himself of in his ability to sense guilt, and he hadn't detected any in Chuck. He may have been a disenchanted husband, but he wasn't into drugs smuggling Tiny was sure of that. As he walked back to his car, he glanced at his wrist watch and was surprised to see it was nearing 4.30 pm. The rumble in his stomach gave him a hint that time was pressing on although the digestive biscuits provided by Chuck combined with those offered by Rawlings earlier in the day, had obscured any desire for lunch. It was a little too early for dinner and lacking the patience to cook, he decided to treat himself to an early supper at the Oakshaw Arms. It was a beautiful day, and it would be good to catch up with a few of the locals whom he hadn't seen since he returned from Ireland. Maybe Rawlings would like to join him, he thought as he approached his Morgan. Rawlings was talking to Paul Chipping outside the stables as Tiny approached. No sooner had he said hello than Paul made his excuses and sauntered off towards the manège. It was clear that he had no time for Tiny.

"You looked deep in conversation?" Tiny prompted.

"Paul was quizzing me about your trip to Ireland; he was very interested but I didn't tell him anything," Rawlings announced proudly.

Tiny smiled. "That's okay. It seems like everyone's interested."

Rawlings was delighted to be asked to supper. He wasn't really hungry but very glad to be back in Tiny's good books. As the Oakshaw Arms didn't open until 6.00 pm, and food wasn't served until 6.30; they agreed to meet at seven. This gave Tiny time to return home and freshen up before taking the short walk across the green to the pub.

Tiny returned to his Morgan, and feeling a little more confident, dropped the hood and set off towards the entrance. Despite Chuck's tale of woe, he actually felt more cheerful than when he arrived. Not only had he restored relations with Rawlings; he had also ruled Chuck out of his investigation, and perhaps more importantly, felt a wave of gratitude for the many happy years he had spent with Patricia.

As Tiny turned onto the main road, he noticed that the familiar black BMW was missing. Despite looking intently all the way home, there was no sight. Tiny wasn't sure whether to feel relieved or worried; he had become quite used to having the company and now strangely felt alone. Better to have your enemy in sight, he thought as he weaved his way through the country lanes back to his home.

Having parked his car, and after raising the hood, he entered his house. As it was still only 5.15 pm, he decided he could just about squeeze in a cuppa and a small slice of Dundee before he needed to head over the green to meet with Rawlings. He sat quietly in his garden with only his thoughts, sipping his tea and savouring every morsel of the moist cake. The garden looked beautiful; the cosmos in the rear of the borders were in full bloom while the begonias and petunias in front ruffled their leaves in the afternoon breeze. With the tea and cake finished, Tiny sat peacefully, his eyes heavy, his breathing shallow.

Tiny was shocked when he awoke and noticed it was already 6.30 pm. He was constantly amazed by how he could while away the hours with only his thoughts for company. Struggling to reactivate his legs after such a peaceful hour, he hobbled into the kitchen with the remnants of his afternoon tea. Still struggling to wake up, he changed his shoes, chose a tie from an informal selection he stored in the downstairs cloakroom, slipped on a light jacket and headed for the door. Checking that he had enough cash to buy a thank-you drink for a few of the locals, he stepped outside, breathed in the warm evening air and headed along the lane towards the pub. It was only about a ten-minute walk which had improved immensely since the arrival of the light evenings and warmer weather.

It was one of those still evenings where a conversation could be heard from a hundred yards away. It was as if life had been put on hold while the sun deepened its glow and gently slipped down the evening sky. The tranquil atmosphere of the evening was suddenly spoilt by the noise of a solitary engine from a car parked some way down the lane. As Tiny approached, his heart sank when he saw it was a dark blue Vauxhall Cavalier. He paused; his nervousness increased as he recalled Rawlings's words earlier in the day. Deciding to take a less direct route, he turned and headed across the green. The car remained stationary, its engine still running.

As Tiny approached the far side of the green, he started to relax a little. The car was still parked; maybe there wasn't a problem after all and he was adding two and two and making five.

He exited the green near Trevor's shop and took a right turn towards the pub. No sooner had he stepped back onto the lane, the dark blue Cavalier screeched away from its parking spot and headed directly towards him. Although only a short distance, it probably reached around forty miles per hour before skidding to a halt in a cloud of dust and the smell of burning rubber. Tiny stood frozen to the spot. It was surreal; he was struggling to process events quickly enough and just couldn't believe what was happening. He was terrified.

The car stopped no more than ten feet from Tiny's position before a thin, blond-haired man jumped from the passenger door. He was holding what appeared to be a hand gun that was suddenly pointing in Tiny's direction.

Within a second, and before either occupant of the Cavalier realised what was happening, a roar of another engine dominated the evening air. From Tiny's left a black BMW appeared at speed, and with no attempt to brake, turned directly into the path of the Cavalier. An almighty crash followed as the BMW struck the Cavalier's off-side wing with considerable force. Both cars lurched towards the green as pieces of bumper, glass and metal flew through the air. Tiny instinctively ducked and remained crouched on the ground, his arms over his head.

As the air cleared, a thickset, grey-haired man pushed his way out of the driver's door of the BMW. The impact had thrown the blond-haired passenger from the Cavalier across the grass, along with his hand gun which was now some distance away. As he regained his composure, he reached out, scrabbling for the gun.

"Leave it!" shouted the man from the BMW. The blond man ignored the warning and with his hand clasp around the grip of his gun, staggered to his feet. Dazed by events, he unwisely raised his arm.

Tiny was deafened by the two gunshots that rang out in quick succession. He could barely look as the blond man was knocked back by the impact of the shots, and lay motionless on the grass, blood pumped pointlessly from two major wounds in his chest. With the noise still ringing in his ears, Tiny could smell the familiar aroma emanating from the discharged weapon. As he opened his eyes and looked up, the sight of a smoking, black, semi-automatic pistol filled his view.

Without hesitation, the man from the BMW swung around before firing two more shots at the driver who was struggling to get out of the damaged Cavalier. Void from dignity, the driver fell into the road, his left leg still caught in the doorway of the car. As his body hit the tarmac, a revolver rolled out of his hand. The whole event was over in seconds. Tiny was still on the ground, his arms held high over his head protecting his ears. With a touch of tenderness, a hand stretched out helping him to his feet. As he looked up into the ashen face of the man from the BMW was stood above him.

"You're okay; you're safe," the man muttered in a deep cockney accent.

Tiny tried to speak, but no words came out. The man guided him to a nearby bench overlooking the green and sat him down.

"I really should be going; I'd rather not hang around to answer too many awkward questions if you know what I mean."

"Who are you?" Tiny stammered.

"I'm no one, I don't exist; but Harry said I should keep an eye on you. Mind you, you certainly get around!" the man responded with a wry smile. With that, he calmly walked back to the road, climbed into his damaged BMW and started to reverse it away from the Cavalier. It took two attempts to separate the cars, but eventually he was free, and with a chunk of the front of his car left on the road, he disappeared around the corner.

There were a few seconds of almost surreal quiet before the mayhem of villagers came rushing towards the green. Sirens could be heard in the distance as the village locals gathered around. The noise of chattering questions was deafening and Tiny was in no mood to answer the recurring 'What happened?' being thrust at him by a horde of concerned locals. He wasn't really sure himself, and was struggling to come to terms with the events that had just occurred.

Within minutes the police were on the scene, and matters started to become a little more ordered. The locals were cleared from the green, 'Police Line: Do Not Cross' tape was erected around the site, and Tiny, who remained on the bench, had a foil blanket draped across his shoulders by a female officer.

"It's for shock," she said. "You're in shock." Like he hadn't realised.

Tiny made no comment, but looked up upon hearing a familiar voice.

"My goodness, never a dull moment with you," Inspector Stock exclaimed, mainly for the benefit of his sergeant who stood next to him looking bewildered by the carnage all around. "I think you should accompany us to the station," he continued. "We have a cosy cell for you and quite a few questions." He added trying to sound impressive.

Before Tiny could respond, a commanding voice took over.

"That's enough, Inspector!"

"Assistant Chief Constable Wilson? ... Sorry, sir, I didn't see you there."

"This is His Honour, Sir Horatio Tiny, one of our country's most prominent High Court judges and you will show him some respect!" Alan barked. "He is the most honourable and honest person I have ever met and he will not 'accompany you to the station'. he mimicked sarcastically. "Do I make myself clear?"

"Yes, sir, of course, sir, ... sorry, sir"

"Now go and do something useful!" Alan commanded. The Inspector and his Sergeant scurried away, trying to put as much distance as possible between themselves and their senior officer.

"Come on, sir, I'll walk you home," Alan reached out his hand and gently guided Tiny to his feet.

As they slowly walked across the green, the throng of police officers moved to one side as if Tiny was parting the Red Sea, each staring at this elderly figure who for some mystifying reason was at the centre of such an extraordinary incident. As Tiny fumbled for his keys, Alan helped him unlock his door.

"From what I remember you have some particularly fine Oban 14?" he suggested gently.

"I thought you would remember that." Responded Tiny starting to regain his sense of humour.

"I think we could both use one, don't you think?"

As they sat in the peace of the drawing room, the events of only a few moments ago seemed almost surreal. Tiny was starting to regain his composure.

"Are you sure you aren't needed out there?" he asked.

"Well… probably, but I expect they can manage for a while. Mind you, the inspector was right about one thing: we do need to ask you a few questions."

"I'm not sure if I can be much help. The chap in the dark blue Cavalier was the Irishman I saw when I was in Galway. The blacksmith over there told me he was a nasty piece of work but I didn't expect this!"

"And the other guy, the one in the black BMW? Do you know him?"

"As I said before, he's been hanging around for a while, but I have no idea of his name."

There was a pause. Tiny was telling the truth, but what he didn't say was probably more important.

"It that it? Nothing more to add?" Alan questioned suspiciously.

"No, not really. There's nothing more I can tell you." Tiny answered, trying to be as honest as he could.

Another rather more awkward pause ensued.

"Well, it's probably a drugs dispute; you've been ruffling feathers, and became caught up between two rival gangs," Alan concluded.

"That sounds like the most plausible explanation to me." Tiny added supportively and with more than a little degree of relief.

"I suppose I should leave you in peace. Besides I should really go and see how the investigation is proceeding. Hopefully there's a couple of competent officers on site by now!"

"The press too no doubt." Tiny added.

"Oh, I expect so. There seems to be an appetite for constant news updates these days, especially the more dramatic stories. Puts us under even more pressure!" Alan answered glumly.

"I don't suppose there's any chance of keeping my name out of the press?"

Alan looked puzzled.

"As you said, I just happened to be in the wrong place at the wrong time."

"I'm not sure that's quite what I said. After all, there must have been some reason why they chose you?"

Alan was far from stupid and Tiny knew it. "It's likely it's tied to the cocaine business and the Ashbury Estate. I'm obviously getting close. My picture splashed all over the front page isn't going to help."

Alan thoughtfully considered Tiny's words. "I'll see what I can do. Maybe I can get a D-notice, but no promises."

"That would be appreciated. Until this is over, the less publicity the better."

As Alan was leaving, he turned and added. "I still think there's more you aren't telling me."

Tiny smiled. "As soon as I'm sure, you will be the first to know."

"Okay, you mind how you go. These people aren't very nice, and they don't play fair, as you discovered this evening."

As Alan was leaving the house, a familiar figure came scurrying down the path in the opposite direction. Alan put out his arm to prevent the visitor from intruding, however Tiny intervened, "It's all right, I know him." As Alan continued on his way, Tiny greeted his guest.

"Mr Rawlings, how good of you to come over. Do come in. I've had a rather busy evening!" He said trying hard to master the understatement. "Come through to the kitchen; I was just about to make some tea."

Although Tiny had great respect for Rawlings, he still rather snobbishly, couldn't bring himself to consider him an equal. Somewhat puzzlingly in its importance, Tiny didn't feel comfortable sharing his drawing room or perhaps more importantly, his most prized Oban 14.

As Tiny closed the front door, the array of blue lights still twinkled prominently in the dwindling light of the evening sky. The two colleagues moved through to the kitchen and sat quietly away from the bustle of the events outside. Rawlings felt privileged to have the sort of relationship with Tiny which meant he could just call in for tea. It was clear that he was hyper-excited about what had happened earlier and began gabbling about various villagers and their speculation on what had happened. The general consensus of opinion appeared to be that was it was a probably a vendetta from a previous criminal case. Wisely Rawlings hadn't commented or offered his more plausible theory, but was keen to find out more details about what actually happened.

Tiny needed to tread carefully. He didn't know how much Rawlings would divulge, probably in all innocence but still, he didn't want to provoke any awkward questions from the locals. Thinking on his feet, he explained that it was probably two rival drug gangs fighting for territory which in a way, he supposed, was sort of true. His enquiries had probably made them nervous and matters must have got out of hand when the other gang became involved.

Rawlings paused; the process of his thought was apparent as he digested Tiny's account of events. Finally, he spoke and agreed that this was probably the most likely scenario. Confident that he now knew the full facts, he finished his tea and headed back to the waiting spectators around the green. A first-hand account from the man himself had to be worth a few pints in the pub.

Tiny smiled to himself as he watched Rawlings hurrying across to his friends. He felt a slight twinge of envy by the non-complicated nature of Rawlings ambitions and wished that he could take such store from the simple pleasures of life.

As Rawlings disappeared into the crowd, Tiny closed the door and once again, he was alone. It was at times like these that he missed Patricia the most. A quiet, empty house was something he had never really got used to, and never really wanted to. He had escaped the bustle of London for a less stressful life, and now look at the chaos and disorder he had caused. Why couldn't he have left matters to the police?

Though all his years on the bench, and before that as a lowly barrister and then as a QC, he had never felt this threatened. Even during the heady years of the war, he couldn't remember feeling fear the way he did right now. Was it his youth back then that had insulated him, and was it now his advancing years that made him feel so vulnerable? Maybe he was still in shock? He couldn't be sure, but he felt powerless, he had no control over events, and for the first time, he felt old.

Chapter Eighteen

As a new dawn gently washed away the dark deeds of the previous day, the village green remained cordoned off. The police were still in attendance, along with a small team of forensic officers, most of whom seemed to be staring at the ground.

Although still a little shaken, Tiny embraced the new day with a renewed sense of positivity. As he thought about the events of the previously evening, he felt almost humbled by what Harry had done for him. It's strange, he thought to himself, sometimes it is those you least expect who turn out to be the ones that help you the most. Mind you, knowing Harry, he doubted if his motives were entirely altruistic.

His thoughts continued to wander, the mystifying facts of the case were finally starting to fall into some sort of order. He paced around the house as he mentally worked on his theory. Although he hoped he was wrong, the evidence seemed to point in one direction, and although he thought he knew who was at the heart of it, he still didn't really know why. Should he tell the police? Probably, but matters had gone too far not to see it through to the end regardless of the consequences. Besides, at the moment all he had was a hypothesis, and until he could present some actual evidence, he was fairly sure his strained relationship with the police wasn't going to improve.

Tiny wandered out onto the terrace and paused as he gazed at his beautiful, tranquil garden. After careful consideration, he concluded that the key lay with the Ashbury Estate. That was where it all started, and every step of the way, it all pointed back to the Estate. With childlike enthusiasm, he decided that was where he should be. First, he needed to check the papers to see if Alan had been successful securing a 'D-notice'. He so hated publicity, and too much attention right now would hinder him. Peering out of the front windows, he couldn't see any members of the press lurking in the bushes. Although encouraging, he knew from experience that restricting their freedom was notoriously difficult. He really didn't want to draw attention to himself and the thought of having reporters camped outside his front door sent shivers down his spine.

Slipping on a pair of deck shoes, he closed the front door behind him and headed across the village towards the shop and post office. Rather than taking the more usual route across the green, he took, what he amusingly called the scenic route to avoid the continuing police investigation and the inevitable throng of onlookers.

As Tiny entered the shop, the familiar tinkle of the bell over the door caused Trevor's head to pop up from behind the counter. Scanning the row of daily newspapers on the counter, the headlines seemed to be dominated by the recent Live Aid concert and the Dutch vote on Europe. Pulling the Times from the rack, Tiny quickly turned to pages, two, three, four then five. There were stories about Andrei Gromyko, the new president of the USSR, the European Space Agency's launch of Giotto to survey Halley's Comet.

There was even an article on thirteen-year-old Ruth Lawrence, the youngest person ever to achieve a first from Oxford University.

Tiny breathed a sigh of relief as he reached into his pocket for some coins. Trevor seemed less happy.

"I'm surprised there no mention of the excitement last night," he said.

"Well, I can't say I'm sorry," Tiny responded.

"Probably too late for the papers." Trevor concluded.

"I expect that's it," Tiny agreed.

Trevor continued, "Tony from the pub was in earlier for extra supplies. He's arranged more staff and reckons with all the press coverage, he going to have a busy few days. Mind you, I'm expecting extra trade too; I could do with shifting some of this stock."

"I hope you're not disappointed." Tiny replied, handing over the money while folding the newspaper and placing it under his arm.

Leaving Trevor rearranging his counter ready for the influx of customers that Tiny secretly hoped would never arrive, he headed back over to Bourne House, quietly grateful for Alan's intervention.

He had been home just long enough to make coffee and settle comfortably in the kitchen when the telephone rang. Making his way to the hall, he picked up the receiver.

Following the usual 'Oakshaw 272' greeting, there was silence. "Hello? Is there anyone there?" he enquired.

"Thanks for keeping it out of the press."

"Harry?"

"Who else did you think it was?"

"Harry, my dear chap, you give me too much credit, but I do want to thank you."

"You're welcome. I thought about what you said, and you were right. My sentence could have been far worse. A favour owed, is now a debt paid."

Tiny didn't quite know how to reply. He paused for a moment before uttering in almost a whisper. "Thank you Harry, it's appreciated," Whilst knowing how inadequate this sounded, he couldn't think what else to say.

"Any time. Mind you, getting rid of another drug dealer is no bad thing,"

Getting rid of a little competition, Tiny thought, then chided himself for being cynical.

"And you just let me know if they bother you again." Harry added.

Tiny replaced the receiver and walked back to the kitchen humbled by Harry's words. It's funny, he thought, how we go through life not really realising how one innocent action can so often have such a profound impact on those around us. Tiny once again sat at the table alone with his thoughts.

It was probably a little after 2.30 pm when Tiny finally decided to visit the Ashbury Estate. Rawlings had mentioned the evening before that Pam was due back, and he was keen to speak with her. It would be a difficult conversation, but he felt quite relaxed, and more like his old self. On-route, he decided he should swing by and update Margaret on the findings of his investigation. Now that he had a little more evidence, he felt confident describing what probably caused the terrible accident that killed Stephen and why the horse behaved as it did. The fact that it was not Stephen's fault should bring his family a little solace he thought and perhaps provide the closure they were so desperately seeking.

Although the weather was dry, the air clear, the sky sunny, it was an uncharacteristically chilly for July so he decided to leave the roof up on his Morgan. As he drove out of the village, he could see the police was finally starting to move the dark blue Cavalier from the green. He was anxious to see it gone; it was a painful reminder of events past and he just wanted everything to return to normal as quickly as possible. He aspired to the quiet life but so far, he hadn't been too successful.

As he turned into the drive of the Ashbury Estate, he almost missed the familiar sight of the black BMW that had accompanied him so diligently over the past few weeks. Knowing now that it had housed his protector rather than his assailant made the absence seem even more profound. Trying to concentrate on the matters ahead, he parked his Morgan in his usual spot before making his way across to the stables.

There was an eerie atmosphere at the yard. Tiny couldn't quite put his finger on what or why, but somehow everything felt different. It seemed deserted. The stables, bar one or two, were empty of their horses. There was no sight of the stable lads, grooms, or staff of any kind. Even Rawlings seemed to be missing, and while he hadn't made any definite arrangement to meet with him, he presumed that his colleague would be somewhere close by. Knowing all too well where assumption leads, he was a little irritated with himself that he hadn't telephoned in advance.

Tiny stood quietly for a while, wondering what to do. Surely there must be someone here, he thought to himself. As he looked around, his puzzlement turned to intrigue. After pacing up and down for another ten minutes, he decided to make his way to the house to speak with Pam, assuming of course, that she was there.

Upon reaching the house, Tiny pulled the cast iron door bell. As he waited patiently on the step, he could hear the familiar 'dingle' from deep inside the house. He didn't really know why, but he felt a slight twinge of nervousness as he stood quietly, his back against the door, awaiting a response. He was wondering whether he should ring again when the heavy oak door slowly swung open with a familiar creak of the hinge.

"Tiny... My goodness, I didn't expect to see you."

Pam stood in the doorway dressed in black trousers and a thin grey woollen short-sleeved top. Her hair was tied back and she looked pale and drawn. The absence of make-up emphasised the lines across her face. Tiny was shocked; the radiant, self-assured beauty he once remembered was absent.

"May I come in?"

Pam just frowned as she stood to one side and ushered Tiny into the hall.

"I could murder a coffee," Tiny commented before realising the insensitively of his comment.

As they walked through to the kitchen, Pam remained silent. Tiny sat at the table while Pam prepared coffee. She sat beside him gently lowering herself onto the chair with elegance and a slight degree of hesitation.

Tiny was the first to break the silence. "Are you on your own."

"Yes," Pam replied in a whisper. "And in more ways than one." Although it was clear that Pam wanted to talk, Tiny was reluctant to probe too deeply into her personal life. He was here for a different reason.

"Chuck's in London, I believe?"

"Yes, he's made it clear that we are no longer together."

"I'm sorry to hear that." Tiny was genuinely sad; over the past few months he had grown fond of both Chuck and Pam.

"He's going to stay in London while he sells the Estate. I received a letter yesterday from his lawyer saying that he had received my application for a divorce."

Tiny paused, he really wasn't sure if he should be encouraging this line of questioning.

"Well, that's a good thing isn't it? Assuming it's what you want?"

"It's not that straightforward." Pam sighed as she placed her elbows on the table and her head in her hands.

"Things rarely are my dear. Am I to assume that your plans haven't worked out quite as you expected?" Tiny responded.

Pam looked up with a worried expression but remained silent.

"So how involved are you?" Tiny enquired, trying to sound matter of fact.

Pam looked horrified. "What do you mean?"

"Oh come on, you are far from innocent in all this. I accept you weren't acting on your own, but you know what's been going on, especially the drugs coming into the yard from Galway."

Pam's face dropped, gently bowing her head, she started to cry. "How did you know?" she sobbed.

"It became clear when I was in Ireland. I caught a glimpse of you in the upstairs window of the house by the sea. But of course, you already know that, because you saw me. There's no way that boat could come ashore, and be stored on site, without you knowing. And as you said nothing, it was clear that you were involved. The only question now, before I call the police, is to what extent"

Placing her hand on Tiny's arm, Pam pleaded. "Oh please, no, you mustn't. I'm so sorry, I'll do anything, but please you mustn't tell anyone."

Whether by her display of raw emotion or maybe because of his own feelings Tiny couldn't be sure, but he was touched.

"But why? Why did you get involved? he asked tenderly.

"I needed the money," Pam blurted through the tears. "Eben said it was harmless and no one would find out. I wanted to build a little nest egg for me and Ian."

"So Ian's also involved?" Tiny was fishing. He had worked out Pam's involvement, and though he knew she had to have an accomplice, he didn't yet understand all the details.

"Ian? Pam looked puzzled. "He wasn't the one who was being bled dry." She added shaking her head. "No, Ian knew nothing about it, at least not until our last trip to Galway. He was horrified, he called me stupid, and now he wants nothing to do with me!" Pam dissolved into floods of tears. Suddenly all the pieces fell into place.

"That makes sense," Tiny said slowly, giving a voice to his thoughts. "Of course, Eben is the international connection, using his local yards as distribution points."

He turned to face Pam. "I still don't understand why you became involved? You say it was for the money, but you have all this." Tiny added, waving his arms around, taking in the room and the entire building in an all-encompassing gesture.

Pam's manner suddenly became hard, cold, almost calculating. "Chuck controlled everything, the money, my life. He even told me what outfits I should wear to impress his friends. I couldn't breathe, I wanted out."

Tiny was shocked by her bitterness.

"But even if you had split up, you wouldn't have walked away with nothing. There was no need to get involved in drugs."

Pam's manner hardened further. "I didn't want a few crumbs; I wanted it all. I wasn't some innocent bystander, you idiot, I organised it: the shipments, the contacts. Do you think I am, some sort of air-head just because I have a pretty face? You are as bad as the rest of them!"

Tiny was speechless, his eyes widened. More than shocked, he was disappointed. How could he have got it so wrong? He had guessed at Pam's involvement, but as the ringleader? Surely not.

"But how about the deaths? Stephen, and Joe Harrison, and the terrible accident at Newbury?" Tiny was scrabbling for answers now.

"Joe Harrison? That slimy weasel! He deserved all he got. Trying to muscle in, demanding a larger cut. Who did he think he was! I never did trust him." Pam's tirade was growing increasingly bitter.

"And how about Stephen and the accident at Newbury?" Tiny asked.

"Just a slight problem with packaging, and that's was Joe's fault too! He really was useless."

232

Tiny had all the information he needed. Although he now knew the identity of Pam's accomplice, he was shocked by the depth of Pam's involvement. Any respect or sympathy he had once had for her had instantly evaporated.

"Accomplice to murder and manslaughter, drug trafficking and distribution... the police are going to love you, especially for what you can tell them about Eben."

Pam's face dropped. The coldness of realisation slowly crept across her body as fear gripped at her very soul.

"I didn't mean for anyone to get hurt. We were just helping satisfy a demand. If users didn't get supplies from us, they would have gone to someone else." Pam was working hard to justify her actions.

"Please!" she pleaded. "I can't go to prison, I really can't."

Tiny sat quietly, watching her sob and beg for leniency.

"Oh, what a mess!" she cried.

"I need to make a phone call." Tiny rose from his chair and walked into the hall. Using the telephone positioned on a small table close to the stairs, he immediately called Alan. After explaining the situation, the ACC insisted on attending the scene personally, and asked Tiny to stay with Pam until they arrived. Tiny agreed, but was in no mood for delays; the sooner he could hand Pam over the better. He went back to the kitchen to sit with Pam before the police arrived only to find that she had vanished. A sense of panic washed over him as he searched room by room without success. Not sure what to do, he paused for a moment to assess the situation; Pam couldn't have left by the front door as she would had to pass through the hall, then it hit him, the back door! Tiny rushed through to the kitchen and into the old boot room behind. He breathed a sigh of relief as he noticed the back door was still locked with the key still on the inside. He was puzzled when he noticed a couple of cupboards of the Welsh dresser had been emptied, their contents strewn across the floor. As he paused to make sense of what he was seeing, he heard footsteps upstairs. Spotting the old servants' staircase on the opposite side of the room, Tiny hurried up the stairs to the landing above. Emerging once again into the daylight, he was greeted by an array of rooms both to his left and to his right. Again, he paused and listened intently. A faint sound of sobbing could be heard emanating from a room at the end of a long corridor. As Tiny made his way towards the room, the sound grew more distinct yet changed in tone to become more laboured.

Tiny made his way down the corridor and gently pushed open the door, conscious that he was probably entering a lady's bedroom. As the door swung open, daylight flooded into the corridor revealing the vision of Pam lying across the bed. Her body was twisted with pain, her head on the pillow, her feet on the floor. An empty cut crystal Old Fashion, glass tumbler lay on its side in the middle of the carpet. A half empty bottle of Jamesons Irish whiskey sat on the bedside cabinet along with a small, orange and red tin, its lid lying on the carpet nearby.

Tiny hurried across to the bed. Pam was disorientated and semi-conscious, her face red and flushed with colour. He lifted her head as he sat on the bed, resting her body in his arms.

"Pam!" he cried. "What have you taken?" Receiving no response, he reached for the tin containing a greyish-white powder, some of which had spilled out over the bedside cabinet. Without his spectacles, and squinting intently, he could just about make out the word Cymag in bold letters. Underneath a black skull and crossbones left little doubt as to purpose of the contents.

Pam's body was limp, her manner distraught, her words incoherent. Traces of white powder could still be seen around her nose and lips. Apart from the occasional 'sorry' between the sobs, Tiny couldn't understand what she was muttering. Her laboured breathing had intensified into a gravely rasp. Her eyes were half closed, her tears mixing awkwardly with saliva from her delirious gabbling. The reality of her suffering disturbed Tiny.

As he held her in his arms, he looked around the room trying to decide what to do. A sense of panic swept over him like a wave swamps a drowning man. Tiny was becoming increasingly distressed as he grappled with the enormity of the situation. His clammy hands tightly gripped Pam as he prayed for life to remain. Repeating kind words and reassurances over and over, his attempts to provide comfort fell into a void of hopelessness. Eventually, a reassuring crescendo of police sirens broke the loneliness.

No sooner had the joy of help lifted Tiny heart, Pam exhaled with a deep, fading, gravel-like breath the likes of which, Tiny had never heard before. Pam's weight seemed to increase as life left the room.

Tiny placed her head on the pillow and hurried downstairs to direct the police. As he reached the hall, the banging on the door intensified. He lifted the latch and pulled it open allowing sunshine to flood the hall.

"Hurry!" he shouted. "She's upstairs in the end room; get an ambulance!"

As two constables dashed up the stairs, another ran towards the patrol car to fetch a medical kit. As the returning policeman pushed past him, Tiny saw Alan walking towards the house, accompanied by two of his senior officers. He stumbled out of the house as Alan approached.

"Tiny! Are you all right, old chap?" Alan asked.

Stumbling over his words, Tiny quickly explained the situation, his voice an octave higher than normal due to the stress. Without responding, all three officers hurried into the house leaving Tiny alone in the serene calmness of a beautiful summer's day. He felt weary, his legs a little wobbly. He sat on the low stone wall next to the door and paused for a moment to catch his breath. Although he knew the police team would make every effort, in his heart, he knew there was little they could do for Pam. As he remained seated, trying to take in events, the peace was shattered by yet more sirens. He looked up to see an ambulance speeding down the drive, blue lights flashing and puffs of dust smoking off its tyres. As it skidded to a halt on the dry gravel, two burly paramedics clambered out clutching oversized bags.

236

They quickly glanced across at Tiny before making their way into the house. Tiny felt there was little more he could do. His thoughts turned to his last conversation with Pam. Her accomplice was still at large, and it wouldn't take long before the news of Pam's demise spread and they vanished forever. This was something Tiny couldn't risk, and though he knew he should stay close by to answer the inevitable questions, he had to act quickly. Justifying matters in his own mind, he turned away from the house and started to walk towards the yard. This was where it all started and Tiny suspected that's where he would find the answers.

Chapter Nineteen

As Tiny approached the yard, he noticed a beige Austin Maestro parked next to the tack room. Although the area still seemed deserted, the car had its rear doors open and was full of bags, saddles and riding equipment. Tiny decided to take a closer look, but as he drew near, he was disturbed by the crunch of footsteps on the gravel.

"Oh, it's you. What do you want? Just nosing around again, I suppose?"

"Hello, Paul," Tiny responded, not rising to the bait. "Are you going somewhere?"

"What's it to do with you? I'll do what whatever I like!" Paul snapped.

Tiny remained calm. "I've just been speaking with Pam."

The colour drained from Paul's face. "Really, and what has she been saying?

"I think you probably know." Paul detected a slight break in Tiny's voice which betrayed his calm demeanour. "I suppose she told you it was all my idea?" he said defensively.

Tiny remained silent.

"Well, it wasn't; she had the connections, reckoned she needed the money, but really, with all this?" Paul responded, gesturing with his arms.

Tiny still remained silent.

"It was her greed that attracted attention. I told her to ease off, but would she listen? Stupid woman!"

"An innocent party, are you? Is that your defence?" Tiny chipped in.

"Well, I'm not as guilty as her, if that's what's she's saying."

"How about Joe Harrison? You can't tell me that was Pam; if you remember she was with me at the time." Tiny added before pausing to let reality sink in, "Besides, a knife isn't really the weapon of a lady."

Paul stared at Tiny, his eyes wide and full of rage. Tiny was suddenly rooted to the spot as he began to appreciate the precarious nature of his situation.

"It was her idea," Paul jabbered on. "Joe was becoming a liability. We couldn't risk drawing attention to ourselves, he had to be stopped."

"So, you thought stabbing him would deflect attention? That wasn't very bright, was it?" Tiny rather unwisely mocked.

In an instant, the atmosphere changed. As the colour returned to Paul's face, he became agitated as beads of sweat started to appear on his brow. Reaching for a dark brown canvass veterinary bag in the rear of the car, Paul pulled out a trocar. Casting the bag aside, Paul gripped its handle and edged towards Tiny, his knuckles white, his fingertips pink with the pressure.

"Joe got was he deserved, and you're as bad. You just couldn't leave it alone, could you? Had to keep interfering. Well, this is where it ends!"

Paul was shaking with rage, red in the face and with teeth gritted, he lunged forward, lashing out towards Tiny's abdomen. Instinctively, Tiny jumped backwards and losing his balance, stumbled before falling to the ground. Before Paul could take advantage of the situation, the tense atmosphere was amplified by a thundering clang.

As the earth-shattering sound of steel ricocheted around the yard like a symbol in the finale of a symphony, Paul crashed to the ground missing Tiny by inches. Tiny struggled to comprehend what had happened. As he looked up in confusion, he saw Rawlings standing over him with a long-handled steel shovel in his hand. Paul lay motionless on the ground, the trocar still in his hand and blood seeping from a wound in the back of his head. With a broad smile, Rawlings stretched out a hand to help Tiny to his feet.

"I heard the commotion and thought you might like some help," he said, leaning the shovel carefully against the Maestro.

Tiny struggled to find any words.

"Never did like the guy," Rawlings added with a broad smile.

"No, indeed. Not a very nice man." Tiny muttered trying to emulate Rawlings talent for understatement.

Neither Tiny or Rawlings were really sure about Paul's condition and at that moment, they didn't really care. As Tiny gathered his thoughts, he realised they needed help.

"Where is everyone?" he asked. "Someone needs to fetch the police."

"Oh, most of the stable lads and grooms have been dismissed, and all but a couple of the horses were shipped out yesterday before Ian left. Paul was just tidying up, and by the looks of things, helping himself to anything he could find."

"I've just been speaking with Alan and his team up at the house."

Rawlings looked puzzled.

"I'll explain later. First, we need an ambulance. Can you give them a call?"

"Of course, I'll be right back." Rawlings replied before scurrying across the yard towards his cottage.

Tiny was alone again. He looked around at the perfect summer scene, manicured lawns, a thousand shades of green amongst the trees, a cloudless, sky. How could the world look so perfect when there was such wretchedness, hate and sadness?

Before Tiny could ponder too deeply, Rawlings was back.

"They are on their way sir, apparently they are quite close by..." Rawlings stopped in mid-sentence as the sight of blue flashing lights drew nearer. "Blimey, they were quick... looks like they were already up at the house." First the ambulance, then a patrol car and finally an unmarked Ford Granada drove into the yard. Alan's entourage surrounded Paul Chipping's body, which lay motionless on the gravel. As the officers beckoned to the paramedics, Alan gently guided Tiny to one side.

"You shouldn't have left the house," he scolded. "And what's going on here? Quite the body count you're stacking up!"

Tiny's breathing was shallow and rapid; he was feeling distinctly nauseous and was plainly looking a little pale.

"Are you all right old chap?" Alan asked. "Do you want to sit down?"

"I'm fine," Tiny assured him, although he knew that was far from the truth. "I assume Pam is dead?" he added.

"Yes; very. She took enough Cymag to kill a horse."

"Cymag? I take it that was the white powder?"

"Yes, farmers use it for pest control, it's basically Cyanide; nasty stuff. You really should get the medical team to check you over especially if you touched it."

"I'm okay, I didn't really touch it and besides, I needed to get to the yard before Paul Chipping made his escape. You know he was Pam's accomplice, he killed Joc Harrison, and nearly killed me. And he would have been successful if Mr Rawlings hadn't intervened."

Before Alan could respond, the familiar sight of Inspector's Stock Sierra arrived, followed by another squad car. Seeing

Alan with Tiny, the inspector, accompanied by Sergeant Niven, decided to concentrate on the scene, which by now, was under the control of Alan's deputies.

The paramedics were busy working on Paul who was now obscured from view. It was however clear from the audible groaning, that he was not dead, well not yet anyway. They had already applied a temporary dressing to his wound and were preparing to move him to the ambulance. Lifting Paul by the shoulders and legs, they rolled him on to the stretcher. As the body turned, the trocar slipped from Paul's hand. For a moment, time froze. Alan caught sight of the weapon and began to piece together the puzzle. After just a few seconds, he looked across at Tiny and nodded. Respect had been restored.

"We need to finish up here," Alan said. "Why don't you go home and have a rest, and then I'll be along for a chat. I will need to take a statement, of course, but that can wait."

"Thank you, Alan I must say, I am feeling rather weary."

"That will be the shock, old chap; perfectly natural."

"Oh... you might want to issue an international warrant for Eben Weller. I think you will find he's the mastermind behind all this.

"Already on it; there's a warrant out for Ian Parkinson too."

"Ian?" Tiny enquired. "He had nothing to do with it, although I truly wish that wasn't the case." He sighed. "Yes, he's a philanderer, and has caused a significant degree of pain and upset, but alas, I regret to conclude, his actions probably weren't criminal."

Alan looked puzzled. "Well, let's sort all that out later. You go home and rest, and I'll call around later this evening. I'm looking forward to sharing your rather excellent malt while you help me fill in the gaps in our investigation." He added with a light-hearted grin.

With that, he turned towards his team, who were still busy cordoning off the area with yet more crime scene tape. The paramedics were loading Paul into the ambulance; he was now sedated for his own protection, and in light of his earlier behaviour, probably for those around him too.

As Tiny made his way back towards his car, he cast his eye around the yard. An officer was climbing into the rear of the ambulance to accompany Paul to the hospital. Sergeant Niven could be heard on the radio requesting SOCO to attend while Alan was deep in conversation with his two deputies.

Tiny still felt a little queasy and was pleased to be leaving. He really hadn't set out today expecting such drama and never thought he would witness the events he had. In such beautiful surroundings, it somehow all seemed a little unreal. Rawlings was revelling in all the attention, and was busy being interviewed by Inspector Stock. Tiny wandered over; he couldn't leave without a word with his old comrade. "Sorry, Matthew, I don't wish to interfere. I just wanted to say goodbye to Mr Rawlings."

"You can't leave the scene until I say so," snapped the inspector.

"Alan's going to call round later to take my statement," Tiny said wearily. "I'm going home for a little rest." He shook Rawlings by the hand. "Thank you, my friend; let's catch up tomorrow for lunch. We can explore the specials board at the Oakshaw Arms, and I'll explain everything."

Rawlings looked shocked. Tiny had never called him a friend before, and although such a small word, it had such an enormous impact. Rawlings just smiled and shook Tiny's hand as a small tear welled in his eye.

The inspector remained silent as Tiny turned away, walked over to his car, dropped the hood and drove away.

Although Tiny had made the return trip to Oakshaw on many occasions, this time it seemed different. The weight of worry had been lifted, the truth aired and the perpetrators exposed. As he weaved his way back home, he revelled in the glow of satisfaction of a job now complete.

As he entered the village, he felt humble, emotional and vulnerable. Catching sight of the church at the western end of the green, he paused, stopped the car and climbed out to take a closer look. Although he wasn't a regular churchgoer, he felt drawn to the entrance. As he walked down the flagstone path towards the heavy oak door, weathered by the passing of time, he paused by a noticeboard headed St Peter's in the Wood written carefully in gold italics. Underneath was a list of the various services offered each Sunday, along with the times, followed at the bottom by 'All welcome'.

These final words somehow resonated with Tiny and remained with him as he gently pushed open the door. Running his fingers over the lichen-covered stone of the fourteenth century chapel, he slowly entered the cool, still air of its interior.

The church, void of a congregation, felt eerie. The atmosphere was peaceful, still and tranquil albeit with a slight feeling of damp and the accompanying smell of old books. With the nave seating no more than forty, the two transepts a further ten each, there was definitely a feeling of intimacy. The apse housed the altar, upon which stood an ornate bronze cross flanked either side by two elaborate unlit candles. Above the altar was the most breathtakingly deep blue stained-glass window portraying St. Peter. Tiny was mesmerised. As he stood in awe, his peace was interrupted by a simple greeting.

"Hello," A man in clerical vestments appeared near silently from the vestry.

"Oh... hello, vicar. I didn't see you there. I hope you don't mind me coming in?"

"Mind? Of course not, everyone's welcome here."

"Thank you, but I thought you might be closed?"

"This is the house of God, it's never closed. If you don't mind me asking, are you Horatio Tiny? I believe you've recently moved into the village?"

"Yes I am. And yes, I haven't been here long."

"You've had a busy time by all accounts," The vicar added. "Is there anything you would like to talk about?"

Tiny considered the offer carefully, and whilst sorely tempted, said only, "Thank you but no. I just wanted a few moments to gather my thoughts."

"Of course, stay as long as you like. I'm off back to the vicarage now but my door is always open. You are welcome at any time."

With a warm smile, the vicar retreated back into the vestry leaving Tiny alone. As he gazed at the altar, his eyes moved again to the stained-glass window above. Finally, he felt at peace.

In the surrounding of such history and permanence, there was a sense of contentment; he had found his sanctuary and for the first time, Oakshaw felt like home.

The End

Printed in Great Britain
by Amazon

57974347R00142